Out of Love

GWENDOLYN CAHILL

Out of Love

TATE PUBLISHING
AND ENTERPRISES, LLC

Published by Tate Publishing & Enterprises, LLC
127 E. Trade Center Terrace | Mustang, Oklahoma 73064 USA
1.888.361.9473 | www.tatepublishing.com

Tate Publishing is committed to excellence in the publishing industry. The company reflects the philosophy established by the founders, based on Psalm 68:11,
"The Lord gave the word and great was the company of those who published it."

Book design copyright © 2016 by Tate Publishing, LLC. All rights reserved.
Cover design by Joshua Rafols
Interior design by Richell Balansag
Author photo by Moises Suriel
Illustration was drawn by Moises Suriel

Published in the United States of America

ISBN: 978-1-68254-220-0
1. Fiction / General
2. Fiction / Crime
15.10.27

DEDICATION

To the memories of my grandparents, Arthur and Bertha Hall Sr., who were on the Deacon and Deaconess Board of Union Baptist Church, a church that is located in New Salem, Pennsylvania.

My mother, who often recited Shakespeare's famous words from *Hamlet*, "To thine own self be true."

My father, whose creative gene continues to live through me.

MACAW

Slowly aroused
From my soporific sleep
Buoyed by the felicitous oratorio
Sung upon the honey coated cords of creation
Planted on the lips
Of the whistling Macaw
Rising to a chorale of serendipity
Whistling comely music
In symphonic harmony
Belting out a chorus
Of crispy notes and rhythm
Spreading delicious joy
Of beauty and reprieve
Serenading beauty
On the stroke of the keys
Pounding out the kinks
On the top of the peak
Spreading precious love
In the forest of Mt. Hope
I am flying to the songs of the sweet Macaw
Pacifying forces

Acknowledgments

I THANK GOD FOR THE gift of song, creativity, joy, and laughter. I also thank Moises Suriel for the beautiful author illustration and Bolanle Adegado whose artwork is featured on the cover. Thank you, Professor Johnnie Woodard of Strayer University, for editorial advice and assistance. Lastly, I thank all who encouraged me to be victorious.

> And the Lord answered me and said, Write the vision and make it plain upon tables, that he may run that readeth it.
>
> —Habakkah 2:2

INTRODUCTION

OUT OF LOVE, AN ADVENTUROUS fictitious love story with many twists and turns, is infused with laughter, drama, determination, sorrow, and triumphs of an African-American couple.

Omari Thomas, a businessman and his partner Susan's successful jazz art boutique empire is suddenly threatened when an expected change in plans leads to an encounter with the dark side of the art business, a world where espionage and white-collar crime quietly dwells.

A wild cab ride from Newark Liberty International Airport suddenly turns their world upside down when an irate cab driver forces them to flee from his cab. Their precious art pieces may never be retrieved from the trunk of the fleeting cab if the police fail to capture the wayward cab driver. The only sight visible on this misty-colored night is the Flame Bar and Grill.

Walk with me as I paint a picture of the emotional upheaval that occurs when the system denies victims due process and justice.

Out of Love has evolved over time and is loosely based on actual events that occurred in the author's life. Art theft often includes a series of illicit crimes including art napping, victimization, drugs, and international intrigue. Robert Volpe, a detective in the NYC Police Department was the first art theft detective in New York City. Volpe was specifically trained in art theft and remained in that position until he resigned in the 1970s.

His investigations required trips to Europe to pursue leads. Art theft ranks third on Europe's and America's list of illicit trade behind illegal sale of drugs and guns. Stolen art pieces are often being found in New York City, a city that is the center of the art world. Many precious art pieces are shipped to New York City primarily from Italy. The theft of art yields billions of dollars of income for professional art thieves.

I invite you to join me on my maiden voyage into the seldom-spoken-about world of art theft, a crime that is seldom resolved.

"You cannot challenge it. It seldom melts into a clear crystal river that rolls smoothly into a bountiful oasis of life. It robs the youth of life and drags others down the cliff barring none from the cell of disaster. It imprisons the very ones who love them and puts a permanent tattoo on the heart of those who are affected. It is white snow, covered in the color of gray. Darkened to the color of black and can lead to unfulfilled dreams. So please don't become a prisoner to the candy that has lead so many astray."

—Gwendolyn Cahill, *Dunbar Blues Away*

In The Beginning

"I'M BLESSED THANK GOD—I'M BLESSED." Omari, who did not look like a man in his early fifties, was dressed in a pair of brown khaki pants and a form-fitting white T-shirt that showed off his muscular body. Omari bounced briskly down the street while joyfully singing. He spotted Afrolena across the street and waved to her. A handful of unopened mail could be seen in Omari's left hand.

Omari walked down his tree-lined street in Newark, New Jersey and continued singing "I won't complain I'm blessed," at the top of his lungs. His baritone voice had an unusual ring. Omari seemed lost in the song until Afrolena shouted out to him from across the street. She burst out into laughter at the sound of his wonderful baritone voice.

Afrolena thought to herself, *there he goes again, lighting up the street with his singing.* "Hey, Omari, did you win the lotto? What do you have in that envelope that you are holding? You're waving that letter in the air like it has gold inside."

Omari continued to wave the letter in the air as he bounced up the stairs to his brownstone. He shouted to Afrolena from the other side of the street—I'll never tell."

Omari, a highly talented male singer, was known throughout the Forest Hill neighborhood in Newark, New Jersey. Omari received his vocal training in a small gospel church that was founded by his grandfather. The historical small wooden framed steeple church with bricks located in a small coal mining town in Pennsylvania also features a small cemetery in their backyard. Omari once wandered into the backyard and marveled at the stone tombstones that resembled the tombstones shown in scary movies. They were crooked, tattered and worn.

"Omari, get out that cemetery, his grandmother shouted. The boogie man might come grab your hand and pull you into one of those graves."

Omari shouted, "Boogie man?" He quickly ran from the melancholic cemetery making sure to remain on the grassy path so as not to step on any of the sleeping bodies.

Omari often sang solos in the Union Baptist Church choir. The unusual architectural design of this African-American church intrigued those who visited the church. The angelic voices of the choir were heard from the choir loft located over the pulpit. The antique wooden pews showed signs of wear and tear. The seats became the temporary home to the small congregation of dedicated church members and visitors.

Omari's ability to hold a tune was noticed when he was four years old. Members of the church heard him sing the church anthem one Sunday and encouraged him to join the choir. He became the youngest member of the Union Baptist Church multi-generational church choir. Every summer Minister Thomas, the proud young pastor of the growing church, eagerly awaited Omari's return to the church. Omari's yearly trek to New Salem, Pennsylvania to visit his grandparents continued until he graduated from high school.

Omari's return to the church was met with a chorus of "Hallelujah, he is home. Hallelujah, hallelujah our star is home." The congregation often burst out into loud shouts of praise when young Omari Thomas stood on his tippy toes to sing into the mic. Inevitably a choir official graciously walked to the podium and handed him the microphone so that he could comfortably sing.

His younger sister, Renee occasionally sang duets with him. She was two years younger than him. Renee's stunning looks and strong vocal range amazed everyone. Omari's older brother Harry, with whom he shared the same birthday, seldom came to Pennsylvania. "Harry was thirteen years older than I. Girls grabbed his attention. That's all he thought about—the girls. Church was not on Harry's to-do list. In fact, he once bragged about scribbling in the hymnals."

Omari moved to Newark, New Jersey to pursue a career in public service. Being a newcomer in unknown territory can be challenging. Omari decided that he needed to find a new church home. An artsy gospel choir billboard located on the side of one of the abandoned brick buildings on Springfield Avenue in Newark captured his eye. The caption on the sign read, New Star Baptist Church: "Strong in Faith, Strong in Voices." Omari decided to attend the church.

The warm atmosphere, friendly smiles, and focus on community services intrigued Omari. There was a strong spiritual aura in the church. When the doors of the church were opened Omari promptly walked down the aisle as the choir sung, "We welcome you, hallelujah." Omari had a bad habit of arriving late to church, he was a night owl from birth.

Omari immediately bonded with the minister and members of New Star Baptist Church. He became a member of the church and singer in their famed gospel choir. Every Sunday, without fail, the choir sang, "Amen." The rich sound of the New Star Baptist Church choir's rendition of "Amen" brought tears to the eyes of the parishioners.

New Star Baptist Church choir competed in Newark's annual McDonald's Gospelfest. This yearly gospel music contest features the voices of more than fifty choirs from the tri-state area participate in this well-known event. Praise dancers, celebrity gospel divas and kings perform at this popular annual event that's held at Prudential Center in Newark, New Jersey. What an awesome feeling it is to sing before a sold out crowd in an arena that holds eighteen thousand people. Omari sang in the highly acclaimed McDonald's Super Choir on a few occasions.

Omari affectionately nicknamed Jill Afrolena because she wore one hell of an afro. Her perfectly shaped, sixties mile high dark brown afro attracted the attention of many. Her natural beauty and powerful stride nearly caused a multi-car accident one day. I'll never forget that day.

A little blush and lipstick did Afrolena well. Her flawless even toned skin was void of blemishes, pimples, and moles. Her natural beauty spoke loudly of the natural beauty of people of color. Jill, a dark-skinned beauty recently turned thirty-five years old.

Her voluptuous curves and fabulous rear end captured the attention of a taxi driver. The taxi driver could not take his eyes off of this curvaceous full-bodied woman who appeared to be five feet-five inches tall. The cab driver came within inches of rear-ending another car. The only thing that prevented him from rear-ending the back of the car was the sudden sound of a steady stream of honking horns.

Omari shouted, "Hey Afro, are you still looking for a job?"

Jill shouted, "Yes."

"I need you to help out in the boutique. I need a receptionist/administrative assistant and an events planner who will be responsible for booking artists and singers for my jazz art boutique. I think you are the perfect candidate. I remember you telling me about your experience in booking talent for college events. Your charisma and warm personality shine. I need a strong vivacious front desk receptionist. Vivacious is your middle name. You will set the tone for the boutique."

The shouting from across the street stopped when Jill finally crossed the street.

Afrolena responded, "Thank you, Omari. I look forward to working at the boutique. How much are you paying?"

"How much do you expect to be paid, Jill?"

"I have no idea. Matter of fact, I don't even know what the market rate is, but twenty-two thousand dollars per year will allow my family to eat, drink, and be merry."

Omari laughed. "This area is expensive. Stop playing yourself cheap. I'll pay you fifty thousand dollars a year and give you 100 percent tuition reimbursement, free medical benefits, two weeks' vacation the first year, and a day added each year thereafter. Plus, you will receive a sick day every month. From time to time, you will travel with me. Of course, all of your traveling expenses will be paid."

"Travel? Oh, say no more! Omari— When do you want me to start? Tomorrow?"

Omari laughed. "You can start on Monday. The hours may vary. For now, I need you to open the boutique at 9:30 a.m. and close around 6:00 p.m. If it is slow, you can close the store at 5:30 p.m." Omari firmly shook Jill's hand.

Jill shouted, "Harambee!"

Omari quickly ran up the ten concrete steps that led to his door step.

Omari opened the ornate wooden door to his well-kept fully furnished one-bedroom apartment, located a few blocks away from Branch Brook Park. His impeccable taste tantalized and intrigued interior designers. The apartment features a plethora of art, designer furniture, precisely placed accessories and a few African artifacts. An eight-by-ten, bright-colored abstract rug welcomed him at the entrance way of his colossal apartment. People were amazed that he did not hire an interior decorator. His eclectic taste included a mixture of Afrocentric art and neo-modern furniture. *Homes of the Elite and Famous* an upscale magazine featured his apartment on their cover. Omari's natural knack for developing interesting interior designs peeked his interest in taking formal courses in interior design at Parson's School of Design. He completed the certificate program last year.

Omari took off his lightweight black trench coat. He tossed his snow-covered boots into the hallway. He sat down at his missionary style desk and opened the mail. He decided to open the letter from the governor's office first. He quickly read the letter. Omari could not believe his eyes. The letter read—

Congratulations! Because of your strong commitment to community service and excellent business practices, the governor of New Jersey will publicly recognize Omari Boutique at the annual awards luncheon. You and a guest are cordially invited to attend the awards ceremony. The event will be held on February 10 in Trenton, NJ. We look forward to seeing you there. Your prompt acknowledgement and acceptance of this prestigious award is greatly appreciated.

Omari shouted with joy, "Yes! This is what I have been striving for." He promptly signed the R.S.V.P. and placed it in the stamped self-addressed envelope.

Omari's hunger finally got the best of him. He walked to the kitchen so that he could re-heat a pot of leftover chicken and dumplings on the stainless stove. Omari was good at cooking. He considered changing his career to culinary arts but decided that cooking was a hobby and not a career path for him. He did not want to become a slave to the kitchen. With his cell phone in his right hand and a spoon in his left, Omari called Susan.

Susan's sultry voice met his ear. "Hello."

"Susan, I received a letter from the governor of New Jersey. Omari Boutique will receive a special commendation for our commitment to community service and excellent business practices."

"That's fabulous," said Susan.

"I want you to come with me to the awards ceremony. The ceremony is being held in Trenton on February 10. I'll pay your way. Your marketing skills have increased our visibility. I need you by my side when I—or should I say we—accept this award. None of this would have been possible without you."

Susan yelled out a loud yes. "I'm packing my bags tonight, Omari."

"Slow down, Susan, the ceremony isn't until February 10th. I was thinking— it's been a while since we travelled together on a business excursion. Perhaps we can extend the trip to another city in the area. I just hired Afrolena.

"Afro who?"

"You know I call my neighbor Jill Afrolena. I am sure she can hold down the fort for a week while we are gone. Her first day of employment will be during the first week of February."

After a few minutes of conversation, they hung up, and Omari immediately called his personal travel agent. "Hi Sonya, I need you to arrange a trip to Trenton for Susan and I. I need two first-class round-trip tickets to Trenton Mercer Airport."

He heard her typing furiously on her keyboard. A few seconds later, she said, "You will have to fly into Philadelphia. The trip from Newark airport is just short of one hour. I can order a limousine from Philadelphia to Trenton, New Jersey. Trenton is thirty-seven minutes away from Philadelphia. Omari, if you invested in a private jet like I suggested you could have flown directly to Trenton Mercer Airport. I am surprised you have not purchased a private jet yet, Omari."

Omari's jovial laughter echoed through the phone lines. "I may be rich, but I am still frugal. In fact, I use the savings on airplane tickets to re-invest in our social responsibility program." Then he rubbed his chin. Flying would be more comfortable if he didn't have to deal with the crowds in the airport.

"Okay Sonya maybe, I'll heed your advice. If our sales continue to soar. I'll finally invest in a private jet." Omari smiled. "I'll finally invest in an on-call pilot next year, but for now, flying first class is enough." When Sonya continued to badger him, he said, "You are crazy Sonya, I'm not that rich."

"Well, you sure fooled me—Come on, Omari, stop lying. You got that fat-cat smile and a thick wallet that I just know is not filled with a stack of dollar bills," responded Susan. Omari laughed.

"Now as I was saying—I reserved a room for you and Susan at the Lafayette Yard Hotel and Conference Center in Trenton, New Jersey. How's that sound, Omari?"

Omari responded, "Perfect. We won't have to travel to another location, the awards ceremony is being held in that hotel too." Then he told Sonya about the letter he received today.

"I always wanted to own a business, Sonya. Finally, my decision to heed the words of my aunt— 'You got to take a chance in life,' has paid off. Lord knows I did not know that the climb to fame and fortune would be wrought with so many snares. Along the way, I caught a number of stars, but I never had intentions of being a star."

Sonya laughed. "Your choice of words always intrigues me Omari. What prompted you to venture into that line of business?"

"Sonya, I have a nature flair with clothing. I decided to present my business plan for a clothing and art business to a venture capitalist. He loved the art gallery plan in my poorly designed business plan. The guy who decided to invest in my dream assured me that he would compose a formal business plan and develop a strong marketing plan." What a mighty fine venture it has been. That was over twenty-five years ago. You see Sonya, I worked full-time but I had a small art business on the side that I quietly cultivated and grew. Within two years of presenting my business plan to the venture capitalist, my business soared. My dream of becoming a full-time entrepreneur finally became a reality.

"I have a fond love for fine art, Sonya. I know that sounds odd, but as you can see, I am a man with many visions. The entrepreneurial spirit lies deep inside of me. My aunt Emily, was the co-owner of McCall's Funeral Home and my cousin Alfred owned a publishing company in the seventies. Cousin Al's thunderous operatic baritone voice awakened the mourning crowd at his father's funeral. That side of my family has Trinidadian roots."

Omari reminisced about the old wise tales and family history. "According to my cousin Edith, who lived in

Teaneck, New Jersey, a relative in our family owned the first black concession stand at Pimlico Racetrack in Baltimore, Maryland. Oh, I forgot—she and her husband, Joe, owned a small pet-fish store in Harlem. Remnants of their fish store remained in their house. Two small glass fish tanks housed a small army of guppies that mesmerized me, as I watched them swim peacefully in a tank free of predators."

"Business ownership is not for everyone. There's plenty of sleepless nights and stress. Unlike fish that are separated from their predators in a glass menagerie, there are tons of predators lurking in the hidden coves in business. But the financial rewards are worth it. I get to call the shots."

"There are invisible chains that bind and hinder people from reaching their full potential. Some people are able to unlock the chains and ease though the holes and snares in this journey called life. But I had dream, a vision and a dime, nothing is going to stop me, Sonya."

"I enjoyed my job as a Child Protective Services worker, but change is good, so they say. CPS number forty was hot. Sixteen years later, I was still in waiting for advancement—stepped out on faith. Lord Jesus forgive me I'd never tell anyone to step out on faith. If you do, make sure you have a path goal leader walking with you."

"I touched a lot of lives, but I realized I reached my self-inflicted glass ceiling. I guess it was God's calling for me to work directly with the people. I took the supervisor's test and passed. I remember how anxiety and my mother's undiagnosed illness led to my suddenly resignation. I also felt that I was called out by God for some unknown calling that would slowly reveal itself to me. My creative gene suddenly burst into full bloom. I was compelled to flee into the world of creativity escapism."

"I reluctantly returned to my job but—things in my life were unsettled. In hindsight, I believe it was the beginning of the philosophical change in political ideology and organizational development. Our freedom to be who we are is slowly being eroded. The melting pot has crumbled. I believe we are witnessing the beginning of the annihilation, denigration, and alienation of the working class."

"I was unable to control my hypertension. One day, I opened the Good Book to a scripture that read 'do not tarry.' I listened to the word. Thank God I did. It was a matter of life or death, so I resigned again. For two long days, I was unable to wake up." "When the Lord tells you your work is done or sends you a word through one of his messengers you better listen," said Omari.

"What's that church saying? 'He may not come when you call him, but he's always on time?' Glory to God, he came right on time. I am alive today because of the Good Book, Hallelujah! Thank you, Jesus! Now I can't say that he has come right on time all the time. Sometimes he lingers in the clouds and throws subtle hints that he has your back. Sonya, I'll be fifty-two years old in February, but I nearly died in my thirties. For two days. I could not wake up. I tried to get up but could not. God brought me through. I can testify to the power of God. Two days… mmm, mmm, mmm, I thank you, Lord. Omari lifted his arms to God."

"I think God wanted me to see life inside of the system, but he could have passed that plate to someone else. When I was forced into the system, my eyes slowly opened. I saw the system from the other side of the table and personally experienced a system engulfed in injustices. The line between clients and employees isn't that wide. Many live just one paycheck away from poverty. I been there I know. The multitude of employment infractions and unfair treatment seemed to multiple. The advancements of yesterday seem to have fallen by the wayside."

He thought back on his experiences. Just when Omari thought he hit rock bottom, he was suddenly hit with another surprise. "My temporary stint on welfare led to my placement in a position that did not require a bachelor's degree. Many educated people found themselves working in positions that they were over-qualified for or perhaps the educational requirement were lowered."

Omari's climb halted. "There's times when you should not take a stepping-stone job. The economy spiraled downward for many. Respect for civil servants and civil service laws seemed to disappear."

"I swear Susan I saw it coming. God sent the vision to me in a dream. Gabriel's trumpet sounded loudly through the air — I tell you, Sonya, I was born to fly. I am not sitting on second base waiting to be flagged on to third. I'm doing a giant leap and sliding into home plate. I dare them to strike me out. The dust is going to fly. I was forced to develop a pliable mind-set."

Well, best-made plans are often wrought in a sea of iron. The doors slammed shut. It was clear that entirely too many things occurred. Omari concluded that the series of incidents that occurred were not blessed by God. It was man's intentional destruction. Omari found himself sprinting like a track and field runner, jumping over hurdles, sometimes scoring, sometimes tripping, and sometimes kicking the hurdles to the ground. One willful act of denial created an avalanche of mass destruction that lasted for well over seven years. It became the catalyst and central theme in Omari's life creating an abyss—. Housing, employment—it was a domino effect. "Omari sighed, "Much like a stack of books falling slowly on a bookshelf, so too fell my life."

Lights, Camera, Action

"Omari, your itinerary to Trenton by way of Philadelphia is finalized," Susan told him after he winded down from a long day at work. "Sonya called. She informed me that she reserved a luxury rental car for us. We will pick up the car at the Philadelphia International Airport. Sonya said we can easily drive to Trenton, from there Omari. She included a few days in Philadelphia. Philadelphia is known for its large public arts displays. The Philadelphia Academy of Fine Arts is well-known. There are a number of art schools and galleries in the area. We have reservations at the Four Seasons Philadelphia hotel. It's a five-star hotel puts one in the mindset of Paris."

"We will depart from Philadelphia on Monday."

"Sounds great, Susan, I have to return to Newark by 9:00 p.m. on Saturday. Bethany Baptist Church's Black History Month celebration is being held on Sunday at the eleven o'clock service. They picked me to sing the solo part in "This Means War." I guess I'll grace them with my presence. Otherwise they will call that other guy. He's not the only singer in the choir."

"Omari, cockiness never fit you," responded Susan in her impudent manner.

"I can sing like him, he's not the only person with that range and pitch. You know who I am talking about. That guy who has a three octave voice that reaches up to the lower range of soprano."

"Sounds like you are jealous, Omari."

"Who me, there's not a jealous bone in my body."

Omari, a professionally recorded tenor, amassed a number of gospel awards, including the prestigious Stellar award. "Come on Sonya, one day I'll have a star on the ground in Hollywood. That's why Bethany Baptist Church called me. They know I can sing."

Bethany is rich in history. It is the first Baptist congregation founded by people of African descent in Newark, New Jersey. The church was formally sanctioned in June 1871. This church cherishes its senior members, education, social justice, and focuses on the needs of churches in other countries. "War is an appropriate song for Newark—that city is known for activism. There's a protest march every week in Newark, New Jersey."

"Let me stop my history lesson."

Omari returned to his newly remodeled gourmet eat-in kitchen. The kitchen contained an upgraded professional stainless steel range, a sub-zero refrigerator, and a center-island counter with a built-in stovetop grill. The smell of freshly grilled chicken and sautéed spinach with garlic filled the room.

"Mmm…that smells good, said Susan."

Omari turned off the stove and served the food. They slowly sipped on Château d' Yquem 1787 sauvignon blanc wine Chateau Yquem 1787 Sauvignon Blanc wine.

"This is delicious Omari."

Omari read the local newspaper while he savored each bit of food. Omari's habit of reading the paper at the dining room table troubled Susan.

"Susan said Omari can't you finish eating and then read the newspaper." Omari ignored her. He stayed on top of the latest developments in local, national, and international news. The day just was not complete unless he read the paper. Omari turned to the advertisements. While turning the pages of the popular local newspaper, Omari noticed the advertisement for the boutique's upcoming jazz concert. He also noticed that his friend's Toyota dealership was about to have a huge President's Day sale. Omari knew that it was time to replace his old car. He grabbed his phone and dialed his friend's number. After five rings he picked up the phone.

"Yo, bro this is Omari. Been a while since I spoke to you. I hope all is well with you and yours. I noticed you have a big car sale advertised in the newspaper. My old car is ready for the junk yard. I need a fully loaded top-of-the-line Camry. I prefer taupe but I will take white."

"This showroom is full of customers. I will get that to you today. My driver will deliver the car to you before the end of the day. As promised Oscar's salesperson, Tim drove the brand new Camry to Omari's home. The car was white with tan leather seats and wood-grain interior, CD/DVD player, handless phone system, sunroof, navigation system with on board Facebook apps and Google apps. It was a custom made car that failed to sell because the customer was suddenly laid-off from his job shortly after he signed the lease.

Omari could well afford to buy a Bentley but he preferred to support his friend's business. The Bible says, "There is one who sticketh closer than a brother." Omari and Oscar built a friendship that weathered all storms.

Omari reminisced about funny moments in his life. Some of his fondest memories included his friendship with Oscar. Oscar Miles and Omari Thomas met each other at college. Oscar and Omari were fraternity line brothers. The brother's in the fraternity nicknamed them "Bop" and "the Whiz." Oscar was branded "the Whiz" of the shows steps, choreography and marketing. Omari's oh-too-cool "bop" lead the line with a swinging bop that serenaded the cheering ladies. The step shows of Omega Phi Upsilon Fraternity brothers yielded high accolades and awards.

After winning a sizeable lawsuit, Miles purchased the car dealership. He spent a half-million dollars in much needed interior and exterior renovations. As a condition of the purchase, Oscar agreed to maintain the current showroom sales staff for a period of one year. Oscar demanded that a

clause be written into the contract that protected his right to change the managerial staff. The former owner of the dealership engaged in a number of shady business tactics. In fact, some of the managerial staff engaged in unsavory business practices.

Oscar renamed the dealership, terminated the dead wood, and employed a top-notch managerial staff. He established an unbreakable rule that any employee found guilty of committing fraudulent acts would be terminated on the spot.

Because of the dealerships tarnished image, a rebranding of the company was necessary. Oscar procured the services of a well-known marketing and public relations firm. The strategic business plan, aimed at increasing brand recognition through an aggressive marketing plan was implemented within thirty days.

Many wondered how Oscar Miles was able to acquire one of the largest dealerships in New York. Oscar inherited a large sum of money when his parents died in a car accident. In addition to monies obtained from the settlement, his inheritance and wise investments lead to him amassing a lucrative portfolio of stocks. Oscar hired the best business attorneys to represent him in an illegal spot deal. His attorney was unbeatable. Even the best of lawyers could not figure out how he managed to purchase the dealership. Once Oscar's attorney became aware of the spot deal, he was determined to win.

The dealership withheld a key from Oscar when they gave him the car. On top of that, one day, Oscar looked out

his window and noticed a tow truck driving up the block. Two black men lurked in the driveway. It just so happened one of the men was the salesperson at the dealership. He wanted Oscar to drive the car to the dealership. Oscar questioned the gentleman about his request.

"Oscar, I left the house door open—can't remember why, but I do remember shoving the salesperson and shouting at him to get off my land when I noticed he was looking at the VIN number."

It has been years since that occurred, but the event remained fresh on his mind.

To make a long story short, the dealership neglected to obtain the auto loan. Two months later, they stole the car from Oscar's driveway. "I remember that day very well, election day. I was supposed to campaign for one of the senatorial candidates."

To say the least Oscar I was so upset he decided not to hand out campaign fliers. From then on it seemed like Oscar encountered Election Day follies every time there was an election.

"Omari I swear, I went to the polls to vote, and the levers were missing from the voting machine. Boy, was I scared. I did not want them to think I stole the G line levers from the machine. It was the year that Al Sharpton and Carl McCall were on the ballot. Their names were on the G line. Carl McCall's failed attempt to become the Governor of New York will always remain in my mind."

"The car fiasco is painted on my mind. I went to the police station, and there was no record of the theft, repossession, or vehicle impoundment notice of the vehicle at the police station."

"What! You lying, Oscar." Omari looked at him in disbelief.

"I kid you not, Omari."

Documents received on the car did not matched up with the Scion xA that he actually purchased. Weeks later, he received a letter from the dealership indicating that his loan was not approved because he could not verify that he had a home owner's insurance on the house that he resided in.

Omari responded, "That is ludicrous Oscar, I can't believe this story."

"You better believe it," responded Oscar.

Oscar's license was suspended for a year because he failed to turn in the plates.

Omari screamed, "What!"

A long pregnant pause proceeded Oscar's next sentence. "These thugs took the car and rode off my land with the plates on the car. There was no way that I could have turned in the plates. My driver's license was suspended for one year."

The DMV counter person showed Oscar a form that the dealership should have completed the form within twenty-four hours of the repossess. A letter to the attorney general resulted in a victorious decision. His lawyer did the rest.

Oscar, a brilliant businessman, who believed in leading by example always checked in with his upper-level

management. On rare occasions he even sold cars in the showroom. His organizational style of leadership was well-received by the staff, management, and the community. Even through the economy was bad, sales at his dealership remained brisk. Oscar's marketing department developed a fabulous strategic marketing and advertising plan. Omari was very impressed with Oscar's marketing plan. He hired Oscar to develop a similar plan for Omari Boutique.

Omari was excited about his new car—so excited that he decided to share his new ride with Susan. Susan became Omari's best friend and confidante. Her ability to analyze and respond in argute dialogue intrigued him.

Omari often visited Susan who recently purchased of a brand new townhouse in Maplewood, New Jersey. He decided to give her a call on Sunday.

"Hey Susan, this is Omari. I know it is the weekend but we need to discuss a few things about the store. I'll come over to your house."

"You can't wait till Monday, Omari?"

"No, Susan this cannot wait. I am on my way."

Omari promptly hung up the phone and jumped in his brand-new car. He arrived safely at her home. He honked the horn and then stood outside of the car. Susan looked out the window. "Just a minute, Omari," she hollered before running out the door. "What's this Omari? I have never seen this car before."

"Surprise! Oscar hooked me up."

"This isn't old car scent smell. This is the real thing, Susan."

"Come on get inside of my new car. I just wanted to show you my new car. Let's go grab a bite to eat in West New York, New Jersey, I need to blow out my engine."

Susan jumped into the car. She immediately kicked off her black high-heeled pump.

"Check out this sound system Susan."

Omari pumped up the volume on his Bose audio system. He put the car on cruise control for the brief ride to West New York, New Jersey. Omari sang along with Sam Cooke's popular tune "You Send Me" when it played on the radio. Omari turned to Susan and, quickly pointed his finger at her. He sang at the top of his lungs, "Susan, you send me. Darling you send me—honest you do honest you do honest you do."

Susan blushed. It was clear that their strictly business partnership suddenly blossomed into a romantic relationship. Omari could no longer hide the fact that he was madly in love with her.

Omari's father was a professionally recorded jazz musician. He played alto sax with many bands including the infamous Snub Mosley band. Lawrence Leo "Snub" Mosley invented the slide saxophone. Omari acquired his father's fond love for all types of music. Omari often rode down the street in this car with his hands bouncing to the beats.

"Something about those beats, Susan—they just go right through me and almost bring me into a trance."

"I am from the old school. My flavor is seventies disco, Mellon's hot mix, Pippins rockers and the sounds of late night male crooners standing outside my window singing in harmony vying for a contract with Motown or Mercury. Give me a little Depeche Mode, Barrington Levy, Nancy Wilson, Led Zepplin, The Jackson Five and Pat Benater. Love really is a battlefield. Crooners rocked my world. But the beats found in hip hop and rap set me off. For me to say that is deep. Marshmallow shoes, afro puffs and hip-hugger bell bottoms represent. Baby boomers are the generation who waved peace signs on a whim. Guns-shots in the night seldom rang out."

"Susan, stick with me Susan. I got big dreams. I just know that one day I will be on the ten top gospel song list. I promise I won't drop you. I think I'll team up with Little Flame."

"Who is Little Flame, Omari?"

"She's a beautiful young rising star who can break the glass with her soprano voice. She'll be a flame to some lucky guy one day. She has a grand career ahead of her.

"Here we are Susan. I love this restaurant. The food is slamming." Omari turned into the professionally landscaped waterfront restaurant parking lot. He purposefully parked his brand-new car in between two spots so that no one would scratch his brand-new car. Susan and Omari enjoyed a leisurely Sunday brunch at the restaurant. In between chews, they discussed an upcoming fundraising event to promote Alzheimer's care and awareness.

As the corporate communications director for Omari Boutique, Susan's duties also included procurement of musical talent for their soon-to-be unveiled gospel brunch concerts and social responsibility programs.

"Alzheimer's in the Hispanic and African-American community is on the rise, Omari."

"I'm glad you agree that this year's fundraiser should focus on Alzheimer's education and awareness. African-American and Hispanics have a higher risk of this disease. Oh, that sounds fabulous, Susan. What raffle prizes are you thinking about giving away?"

"A car. I am sure that your friend, Oscar, would love to promote his Toyota dealership. Perhaps he will allow us to give away one of the cars."

"That sounds like a fabulous idea Susan. I am sure that Oscar Miles will be happy to partner with us. It will also increase his visibility and strengthen brand loyalty. That's a win-win situation. For second prize perhaps my friend who owns a travel agency will donate a trip for two to Nassau. He always looks for innovative ways to market his business."

Than the talk turned to Omari Boutique.

"Susan, our growth at Omari Boutique is phenomenal. Due to our growth, I have decided to hire Afrolena. She can begin working at the store when we go on the trip to Trenton. I'll train her before we leave. In February, we are going to expand our art displays. I think we should feature the phenomenal artwork of Moises Suriel, Nigerian artist Bolanle Adeboye and the art of local artists." The exhibit can be entitled *Out of Love*. Susan's excitement could not be contained. "That sounds like a great idea, Omari."

The gallery developed a strong following. The boutique's wonderful collection of fine African diaspora art, live music, and guest speakers attracted artists, businessmen and famous people. People would soon be able to eat, chat, and network in an intimate café atmosphere. The store, located in a high-traffic area in Newark, New Jersey was within walking distance to NJPAC.

"I need you to develop a classy soiree with a relatively well-known guest speaker and live music for the Grand Opening. I want you to be my partner, Susan. I have grand plans for Omari Boutique. Within two years, I plan to expand Omari Boutique to Brooklyn, New York. Five years later I am going to open a branch in Richmond."

"Our online Omari Boutique bridal division is booming. Our decision to focus on the needs of the over forty, full-figured women paid off. I think we should open a clothing store and small cafe in our next Omari Boutique store. We can develop an African bridal line and fashion show. The convertible mud-cloth body length cathedral train wedding gown can be featured in the show. This grown is a show stopper. After the wedding ceremony is over the bride can untie the train from her waist and than wear the train as a cap This symbolic gesture indicates that the bride and groom tied the knot. This wedding gown flatters all figures and is fashion trendy. I'm already lining up a number of professional models for the show."

A brilliant smile painted across Susan's face. Memories of a fashion show that Susan and her college classmates coordinated danced across her mind. The theme was based on the "*Night Fever* movie." Susan chuckled as she reminisced about the various scenes in the fashion show.

"We crossed the 'barely there' line when one of the coordinators wore a sheer black night gown that showed her breasts."

She was the sexy full-figured model that everyone loved.

"That's right, I'm a former disco diva and proud of it. I got your electric slide—That is just the bus stop in disguise. Hustle baby hustle."

Omari laughed. "Baby, I love you, and I adore your wonderful sense of humor."

He gently blew a kiss into Susan's ear while reaching into his pocket. Omari suddenly got down on his knees. He opened a small ring box. Susan gasped for air.

"Susan, I want you to be my wife."

Omari's conspicuous action lead to a symphony of claps and screams from the patrons at the restaurant.

Susan's eyes widened when she saw the flawless two carat diamond ring in the box. One of the patrons yelled say yes. Susan graciously accepted his offer.

The maître d' wheeled in an ornate silver wine bucket that contained a bottle of Dom Perignon champagne. "In celebration of your engagement the management and staff of Jerkwater present to you a free bottle of champagne."

FLAME BAR AND GRILL

SUSAN WAS CONCEIVED AND BORN in Nigeria. Her parents were on a sabbatical from their respective positions as faculty members of New York University. They were offered fellowships through the prestigious Thomas R. Pickering Foreign Affairs program. A paid internship in Nigeria lead to their re-location to Nigeria. Upon completion of the program her parents were required to fulfill their contractual agreement to become Foreign Affairs officers for a minimum of five years. Nine months after their arrival, Susan was born. Their two-year sabbatical ended up being a ten-year residency in Nigeria. They fell in love with the people and culture of Africa.

They explored Nigerian culture so that they could develop a book on the growing AIDS epidemic. Susan became fluent in Yoruba and English. She was eleven years old when they returned to the States.

Susan was raised in a traditional Christian family that stressed high morals and integrity. Susan's dark brown skin often captured the steady gaze of men. Her six feet tall curvaceous body plus striking looks commanded the attention of the paparazzi. Susan's well-chiseled cheek bones, full lips, and thick brown, shoulder-length hair gently framed her face.

Omari longed to visit the motherland one day. Susan spoke so warmly about the country. She educated Omari about the history of her homeland.

"Lagos is no longer the capital of Nigeria. The capital was moved in 1991 to Abuja. My country is rich in oil, coca, peanuts, corn, rice, sorghum, rubber, and goats. There are two major rivers that run through Nigeria, the Niger and the Benue. From these rivers flow many small rivers and creeks."

"The five primary languages spoken in Nigeria are English, Hausa, Yoruba, Igbo, and Fulani. Unfortunately, the life expectancy of we Nigerians is far below that of Americans."

"Hold up, Susan, you said 'we Nigerians.' That's an interesting statement, Susan."

"I adopted the culture. I was born in Nigeria and have dual citizenship with Nigeria and America. Omari, don't interrupt the history lesson."

Omari chuckled.

"Now as I was saying, the average life expectancy is fifty years of age. The primary religions practiced in Nigeria are Muslim and Christianity. "Many people born in Africa carry the beginning name of *Olu*, which means "God," followed by another meaningful name. There are approximately 250 ethnic groups in Nigeria. Nigeria is the most populous country in Africa. Nigeria has a very strong global economy. In fact, China is number 1 in global economics, and Nigeria is number 2."

"I'm sure that my contacts in Africa will be happy to assist in the development of an upscale African bridal apparel line, Omari. I remember you mentioning in passing that you have an interest in developing a bridal line. Thanks to the Nigerian trade agreement, American companies who engage in trade with Africa can reap the rewards of tax benefits and grant opportunities. Perhaps we should begin to put that vision in motion. We can have the clothing manufactured in Nigeria for a fraction of the cost of garments made in America. I am in the midst of trademarking a design that can be used as a bridal label. We can use the trademark in the bridal line."

"That is a wonderful idea, Susan."

Susan's enrollment in the NYU Stern School of Business paid off. Her brilliant business mind could not be surpassed. Upon graduating from the Stern School for Business, Susan enrolled in NYU's international relations graduate certificate program.

Susan loved art. By the time Susan reached the third grade her creative talents in musical instruments and drawing became apparent to her parents and teachers. In Susan's spare time, she developed computer art cartoon designs that featured Afrocentric designs and figures. Most of her illustrations consisted of cartoon drawings that featured strong African facial features.

Susan realized that her art should be marketed in Africa. She wanted to develop a small core of talented illustrators for a publishing company. However, after taking two courses in publishing, she realized that the publishing business was not the right track for her. Omari's vision of incorporating international art purchases in the boutique interested her. In time they formed a business partnership.

Jill could not wait till Monday. It was Friday, and she was counting down the hours to her first day of work at Omari Boutique. She thought back to when she first met Omari. She was the head of the charity event. Funds raised from the event were presented to a neighborhood homeless shelter. Jill's collaborative fund raising event was sponsored by Omari Boutique. Omari's company's philosophy of giving back to the community blended well with Jill's desire to give back to her community. This endeavor brought increased visibility and traffic into Omari Boutique. Omari was impressed with her work. The joint venture led to Omari's decision to hire her.

Saturday began with a trip to Omari Boutique for training on the operational practices of the store. Sunday morning worship proved to be enlightening. The sermon was based on Proverbs 19:17. It was Easter Sunday, ladies and gents dressed in fine wear shouted Hallelujah! The choir begun the worship service with, "I Had a Talk with God." Jill sang in the choir—an intergenerational choir that consisted of fifty singers.

The sermon spoke to her heart.

Susan reminisced about her foot soldier days. She marched in a number of high-profile protests in New York City, Newark and DC. The marches she participated in included, the Sean Bell protest, reclaim the dream protest against a cartoon that appeared in a well-known NYC newspaper and a few marches in Newark, NJ.

There were dangers involved in being a foot soldier. Jill was nearly crushed in a protest march when she participated in the march against a 2009 cartoon that appeared in the *New York Post*. An unknown man decided it was cute to walk backwards on the protest line.

Jill returned from church renewed. The day went quickly. She laid out an outfit for her first day of work. She decided to wear a casual-chic Kente clothe outfit to work. She kissed her children, Rose and Eric, good night and tucked them tightly in the bed.

The next morning, Jill walked from the subway station to work. She spotted a small donut shop known for their wide assortment of freshly baked pastries and donuts. Jill ordered a medium coffee, regular, two sugars and cream, and a glazed donut. While waiting for her order Jill noticed a handsome man with shaded glasses standing at the counter looking at her like he saw Jesus. Jill quickly turned to the cashier and paid for her order. Jill scurried out the door and continued to walk a half a block to the store with her brown paper bag in hand. She unlocked the door and checked the phone messages and turned on the stereo system. Jill received her first phone call at 9:15 a.m.

She decided to call Omari to set his mind at ease, "Hey, Omari, this is Jill. I'm just calling to let you know everything is fine at the gallery. Sales have been brisk."

"Susan and I arrived at Newark Airport on time for the flight to Philadelphia. We purchased a few new art pieces for the store. I'm sure you will love what we picked. I can't wait to show you the items. I also found two bronze statues. One is light enough to carry on the plane. The other statue is too heavy to carry. The store is shipping it to the boutique. It might arrive at the store before we return home so please be on the lookout for the FedEx delivery."

"No problem, Omari."

"Tomorrow is the luncheon. I'll call you after the ceremony. You have any questions?"

"No, Omari, enjoy your trip."

"I'll talk to you tomorrow, Jill. Stay safe."

The awards luncheon and ceremony was filled with politicians, celebrities, and well-known sports figures. This event garnered the attention of the press, local television, and radio stations. Omari gleefully walked to the podium. He graciously accepted the governor's corporate responsibility award for Omari Boutique, a company that also employed individuals in the community.

"Thank you. None of this would be possible without my partner and fiancée, Susan, with whom I am sharing this award."

The governor suggested that Susan come to the stage. She wore a beautiful Dana Buchman pantsuit. The sound of clicking cameras and sight of flashing lights filled the room. They were hot, and for whatever reason, strangers could see that there was a special chemistry between them, one that commanded the attention of the media.

Omari phoned the store. "Omari stop worrying everything is fine. Business is brisk today I have a room full of customers I need to get off the phone."

"Okay, take care, Afrolena."

Back at the boutique, two well-dressed men arrived at the reception desk. They looked at the art on the wall.

"These art pieces are lovely. The store design is glamorous—definitely user-friendly."

The boutique also housed a self-service computer station and frame shop. Customers were able to explore their extensive art collection and place orders. Some of Susan's art was also featured on their website.

A list of upcoming events was posted on the neon easel. A number of customers dined and enjoyed the softly piped in jazz music that played in the Omari Boutique Café. One of the well-suited men handed Afrolena a business card. Afrolena glanced at the card.

"Oh, you represent a major television network. I'll refer this to our in-house corporate communication officer."

Omari advised Afrolena prior to their departure that all inquiries from the press should be presented to Susan. Afrolena attempted to call Omari, but she was redirected to his voice mail.

"Mr. Lynton from WCDQ would like you to call him," said Afrolena in her soft voice."

Upon receipt of the message, Omari immediately returned the call to Afrolena.

"Jill, you forgot to leave his phone number on the voice mail."

"I'm sorry. All of a sudden, things got busy in here. I need to talk to you anyway, Omari. I have a very large order here and would like to know if you can access the computer to ensure that we can expedite this order."

Omari remotely accessed the order on his cell phone. Someone placed an order for a number of Susan's art work.

"This is a sizeable order."

Omari assured Afrolena that the order was properly coded and could be delivered to the store within three days.

"Thanks, Omari."

Susan returned Mr. Lynton's phone call.

"Hello, Susan, I am so happy to hear from you. I enjoyed visiting your boutique today. Our television network WCDQ would like to feature the store. We are developing a series on art boutiques. You have developed a unique niche. We love the vibe in your urban chic boutique.

"Mr. Lynton, Omari and I will return to New York City in three days. I would love to meet with Mr. Lynton. How does Tuesday at 2:00 p.m. sound?"

"That sounds fine, Susan. We want to feature your boutique on a show that is scheduled to air in the fall."

Susan put the call on a conference call so that she would not have to repeat the information. Omari was delighted. Omari shouted. "I'll tell Jill to send information about our company to you via e-mail."

"We would like to videotape the boutique on Tuesday. We will bring the camera crew with us."

"That sounds fine," said Omari.

Omari hung up the phone and shouted. "Yes! Thank you Jesus. We are going on national television."

Susan warmly embraced Omari and walked hand in hand with him as they viewed the wonderful sights of Philadelphia. They thoroughly enjoyed the galleries. They purchased a few fine art paintings and two rare bronze statues. The six-foot-tall bronze statue was shipped directly to the boutique from the art gallery. Susan and Omari enjoyed the sights of Philadelphia but they were eager to return to Newark, New Jersey.

The flight home was rocky. The turbulent skies were full of dark clouds and lightning. Susan lay her head on Omari's shoulder during much of the ride until a bolt of lightning jolted her from her sleep.

"What on earth was that, Omari?"

"I don't know how you slept so solidly this far. It seems we have been flying through this major storm front for at least twenty minutes."

The captain announced, "We expect to land at Newark Liberty International Airport in ten minutes. Please fasten your seat belts."

Susan gathered her books and placed them into her carry-on bag, which she slid underneath the seat. The plane flew through the last storm cloud and entered into dry skies. Upon departing from the plane, they immediately claimed their luggage from baggage claim.

A limousine was scheduled to pick up Susan and Omari at Newark Liberty International airport at 4:00 p.m.; however, the weather delayed their arrival. Omari asked the limo company to change the pick-up time to five o'clock, but due to weather conditions, the company was unable to accommodate them.

Omari was livid. "Man, you know I am a good paying customer. I can't believe you have no one to transport us home."

"I am sorry, Omari. Many of our drivers did not come in. You can call this phone number. I am sure they will be able to accommodate you."

Omari phoned the number given to him. "No problem, a cab is already at the airport. I'll re-direct him to you. Which terminal are you at, asked the dispatcher?"

"We're in the Jet Blue terminal. We are standing in the baggage claim area."

The taxicab driver stood at the end of the baggage area with a placard in his hand. The driver directed them to his cab and placed their items in the trunk. He slowly departed from the curb.

Susan refreshed her worn-off lipstick. "I know one thing; I am happy we are home." The taxicab driver took a sudden sharp left turn out of the terminal and sped down the street. "These roads are icy. Please slow down."

The driver did not even look at Omari, and he drove toward Jersey City instead of Newark.

Susan was horrified. "Omari—Omari what's wrong with this driver?"

"Hey, man, where you driving us to? You are driving like you in some speed derby. We are in no hurry. We want to arrive safely," said Omari.

The driver turned around and said, "Shut up you. You are on my time, and I drive you to where I want to go."

The odometer read eighty miles an hour, and there was no way out.

"Yo man, I said stop the car."

"Shut up. I said shut up," yelled the irate cab driver."

"No man. What do you want? I will pay you now to stop this car," said Omari.

The car exited the highway at high speed. The driver swerved on a patch of ice, nearly hitting a pedestrian who was walking a dog on a leash.

"Hey," shouted Susan.

Omari noticed a police car across the street, but the police car continued on with its siren and flashing lights.

The crazed cab driver continued to drive wildly down the snow lined barren streets. He slammed on the brakes and came to an abrupt halt at the Jersey City waterfront.

Omari noticed a police car across the street, but the police car continued on with its sirens and flashing lights on.

The sudden stop jerked Susan and Omari forward. Susan nearly hit the glass panel that separates the driver from the passenger.

"Hey man, you riding on ecstasy or maybe even crack."

"Get out," shouted the taxi driver from the front seat of the cab, "Get out now."

"Okay man, we're out of here," shouted Omari.

The driver shouted from the window as he drove away, "You're lucky I did not kill you."

Susan screamed. "He stole the art. Omari, the art is in the cab."

Omari grabbed Susan's hand. They ran to a nearby wooded area. Omari occasionally glanced back at the fleeting cab. He observed the driver farther and then suddenly slam on the brakes and get out the cab. The driver ran wildly to the trunk of the cab, popped it open, and haphazardly flung Susan's and Omari's items but he "neglected" to remove the art from the trunk of the cab.

Omari breathed heavily as he shouted, "Oh my God. That art is worth two million dollars, shouted Omari." Omari admitted he had no intentions of placing the Picasso in the galley.

"I brought that for us."

"I was wondering why you did not buy African art, said Susan."

They silently watched the speeding cab drive away. One could tell by the stoic look on Susan's face that she was totally befuddled by the events that just occurred. Susan and Omari stood in the middle of nowhere. The night was hazy, and the air was covered by a thick cloud of dust. Finally, they were able to peek through a clearing in the air.

"Where are we, Omari?"

"I don't know where we are Susan, but I can see the Jersey City waterfront."

Susan quickly pointed to a building that peeked through a clearing in the fog covered night. "Look over there. There appears to be a lonesome bar standing alone on a barren strip of land. I can barely make out the name on the sign."

She squinted her eyes. "The name of the bar on the neon-lit sign reads the Flame Bar and Grill."

Omari responded, "That's a well-known restaurant in Jersey City. I'm sure the police will be able to locate us now." Omari pulled his cell phone out his pants pocket. "Susan, the juice has died on my cell phone. Is your cell phone working?"

Susan nervously searched through her handbag and found her phone. Her hands trembled as she phoned 911. They attempted to see the license plate number on the cab as it drove away, but the thick mist of gray haze and fog obscured their view. The police were able to quickly pinpoint Susan and Omari. Susan notified the dispatcher that she observed The Flame Bar and Grill's neon sign.

Before long, they heard a siren and saw a police car headed in their direction. The police officer immediately recognized Susan and Omari, as he purchased a number of items from Omari Boutique.

"Hi, Officer Jones we are glad to see you."

"So what happened, Omari?" asked Officer Jones?

Omari explained exactly what happened.

"So in a nutshell, you are telling me that a cab driver tossed you out the car and drove you off the beaten path?" said Officer Jones.

"Yep, in a nutshell that is exactly what occurred," said Susan. "We were unable to see the license plate. I only got the first three letters of the license plate— EBE."

"Can you describe the driver?"

"He was about five feet eight inches tall and thin. He appeared to be white. He was dressed in casual clothing—white T-shirt and blue jeans. He has a slight tan. One could see the definitive tan line on his arm."

Officer Jones responded, "That is very interesting, being that it is February. It sounds like this guy recently returned from a vacation or does not live here."

"What was the name of the cab company, Omari?"

"I'm having a temporary lapse in memory. Let me think. I can see the sign neatly painted on the driver's side of the door. Officer, I'm still a bit shaken up from this. I remember now. It was Premium Cab, and the car number 378 was painted on the back of the car. As the car sped away, I noticed the numbers. I have always had a thing for numbers, even though I was terrible in math."

"I need you to come into the police station so that we can submit a formal complaint. Did you lose any items?"

"Yes, a few expensive paintings were in the trunk of the cab. Luckily we insured the items in Philadelphia. Those paintings and the statue are priceless. The value of the three items is close to three million dollars. The Picasso alone cost two million dollars."

"I hate to tell you, Omari, but this sounds like a set-up."

Omari's face dropped. The painful look of shock now painted on his face spoke volumes.

"Who made these arrangements for you?"

Susan responded. "Our usual limo company was unable to accommodate us, so the company suggested that they use Premium Cab."

"I suggest that you not use that limo company again. It sounds like an inside job to me," said Officer Jones. Officer Mark Jones quickly patched the information about the driver and the license plate to the central dispatcher. An all-points alert was sent to all officers in the immediate area of the crime. It was reported that a yellow cab was spotted parked on the side of the road, approximately ten miles north of the place where Susan and Omari were abruptly forced to depart from the cab. The engine was still running. The sign on the cab read Premium Cab.

"We got a hot lead here. Someone spotted the suspect in the vicinity of Freedom Way and Audrey Zapp Drive. I need back-up. This is a case of art theft. This car fits the description. The New York license plate contains the letters EBE, and it is a Premium cab."

Officer Jones and his partner, Officer Manley, were advised to approach the idling vehicle with caution. From a distance, it appeared as though no one was inside the car. As the officers drove closer to the car, a white man with a tan bobbed up from the front seat and brandished a gun. Much like the birds who swoop their prey, a caravan of police cars swooped down upon the criminals.

The officers with guns drawn, immediately shouted, "Drop your gun." Instead, a hail of gunfire erupted from the armed gunman. The officers returned fire.

The unknown assailant pumped another round of bullets at the officers as he ran out of the car. One policeman down, four officers pursued the armed gunman on foot. One of the officers twisted his ankle while running and fell to the ground. He writhed in pain while the others continued the pursuit. The suspect ran to the wooded area of Liberty State Park. He dodged and cowered into the bushes before running to the shore. The sudden sound of splashing water resonated through the air. The suspect swiftly jumped with ease into the frigid waters of the Hudson River. He swam expeditiously to a boat that stood still on the choppy waters of the Hudson River.

The police helicopter hovered over the small boat while uniformed officers holding high power machine guns engulfed the crime scene. The NYC/NJ Harbor Patrol was summoned to the scene of the crime. Searchlights from various NYC/ NJ Police helicopters shined brightly on the boat. Just as the assailant placed his hands on the railing of the boat, an earsplitting cry and a sudden splash of the water sent Navy Seals into the murky colored Hudson River water.

The NYC/NJ Police helicopter easily penetrated the thick, hazy skies. The man in the helicopter pulled the trigger, aimed, and landed a flawless shot that sailed through the hazy sky. One bullet was all it took to snuff the life out of this two-bit scum. The shot immediately pierced the man's heart. The body was quickly retrieved from the water.

"Halt!" screamed the police over the loudspeaker, to the pilot of the boat. Sensing that he would not escape, the pilot of the boat immediately sent a text message to an unknown person.

He immediately stood up from the steering wheel of the boat with his hands in the air. The pilot shouted, "I surrender." He knew there was no way out. He was not prepared to die tonight.

Police searched the boat. They immediately identified him as Pedro Nimo. They found nothing unusual in the boat. They charged him with aiding and abetting. The boat was registered to a third party company.

The police were able to retrieve the driver's license from the dead man's body. The photo on the driver's license verified the victim's name, John Turner.

Omari and Susan were relieved. The police informed them that the suspect has been located. "You will be happy to know that your items were retrieved from the trunk of the cab.

"All of our items?"

"Yes, Omari."

John Turner was thirty-two years old when he died in the muddy waters of the Hudson River.

Pedro confessed, "It was an attempted kidnapping." "I knew their flight time and conspired with Express limousine to kidnap them. Express agreed to reroute Susan and Omari to Premium. If the kidnapping was successfully executed, Premium would pay me a substantial monetary reward. Limousine Company received a small advance."

Officer Manley asked Pedro, "What was the motive? Come on, punk, answer the question."

"I need a lawyer," Pedro screamed.

"You sure do Pedro. Who owns this boat?"

Pedro skirted around the question. "Premium needed a large sum of money to pay off a loan they obtained from a loan shark, so they took a bribe from Express Limousine, LLC to pay off the loan. Express is the number 1 limo company in the area. That company dominates the marketplace. That empire is worth one hundred million dollars. Express limo is a cash cow. They are not hurting for cash. In fact, Express needed to dump a little excess cash. My hand was empty. I got a family. They like to eat. I received a substantial advance from Express. I was on my way to stardom when you shot me down."

Pedro shouted, "I need a lawyer."

"Who are you screaming at, Pedro?"

The officer then shoved him on his back, nearly knocking him to the ground. Pedro screamed in pain. One could see that Pedro was now out of breath and thrashing in pain. The commanding officer shouted "Order the strip search, You're a mule aren't you?"

"Who owns the boat?"

"I need to go to the bathroom."

"No, you can sit in that chair until you urinate on yourself—Answer the question punk."

"I need a lawyer," shouted Pedro.

"I own the boat."

"You're lying punk."

"I own the boat. That is my company."

"You just said you needed money to feed your family."

"Look man I told you a lot," said Pedro."

"Go do your research, Officer."

"Yo, who you think you talking to, Pedro?

I can make this mighty uncomfortable for you." An officer in the crowded interrogation removed the soft handcuffs from his wrist and replaced the handcuffs with metal handcuffs.

Pedro screamed in pain. Blood slowly tickled down his hand. "I told you man that's my company, I am a fisherman. But I needed more money to sustain the company. We were going to sell the paintings and than purchase a large supply of drugs to sell on the street. Than it was our intention to call your assistant at Omari Boutique to demand money for the return of Susan and Omari."

A strip search of his body revealed that Pedro had a substantial amount of drugs lodged in his anus.

"Who is your supplier?"

Pedro refused to respond. A ton of officers surrounded him.

"Hey punk, 'who was your supplier?'"

The police were already in possession of his personal property. A small amount of cocaine was found in his pocket. One of the officers swung the bag of coke in the air and said, "You see this dangling bag of coke? Well this is what I will do to you if you don't answer the questions. This bag of coke is going to hang you."

One of the officers shoved him. Another one hit him with his hand. Pedro sustained a few bruises before he broke his silence.

All right! shouted Pedro. "I want a lawyer; I know my rights."

You can check the numbers on the phone if you want to find out who the supplier is."

One officer responded "You'll get a lawyer when we decide you can get one. In the meantime, you have the right…"

The police chief recognized the number immediately. This guy is connected to a major drug cartel. Pedro was booked and charged as an accomplice in the attempted kidnapping of Omari and Susan. He was charged with illegal possession of drugs. The police would continue to investigate the company that was allegedly owned by Pedro. Police figured there was a larger picture that might unfold.

Meanwhile, in another room, Officer Jones asked Omari if there were any other unusual incidents at the boutique. Omari said, well three days before we were scheduled to return, I received a call from my receptionist. She informed me that two men from WCDQ wanted to film the store for an upcoming story on art boutiques."

"We need the names of these guys."

Omari called Jill. "Hey, Jill. Please fax copies of the business cards from the WCDQ representative so I can give this information to the police." "I don't have time to explain."

Jill was shocked. "Are you guys all right? You are at a police station? Where?"

"Jill, we are fine. We are in New Jersey. I'll explain what happened later. Please fax the business cards to Officer Manley at this fax number."

The police advised Omari that they were going to do a background check on the WCDQ representatives. "We need to investigate the legitimacy of these representatives," said Officer Manley.

The police advised Susan and Omari that they should cancel the photo shoot. Omari attempted to phone Mr. Lynton, the representative, for WCDQ's phone number.

A recording came on: "The number you have reached has been disconnected."

Omari phoned the number again to confirm that he dialed the correct phone number. The same recording came on, "The number you are trying to reach is no longer in service."

Omari called Manley, "You can check it for yourself, Manley. Lynton's number is no longer in service."

After a long night of interviews, unexpected twists, and big-time drama, Susan and Omari completed the crime complaint form for victims and signed it. They quickly departed from the precinct.

Omari and Susan returned to Omari's apartment. Omari unpacked his Louie Vuitton suitcase. Susan dreaded the thought of having to return to her Plainfield home after the fiasco. "Omari, I would like to spend the night with you. I'm tired, I just do not want to be alone tonight."

"Susan, I do not expect you to go home tonight. In fact, now that we are engaged, we will have to discuss where we will live, but tonight, I just want to unwind. I told you, I want you to be my partner for life. Hey, honey, I've got some wine in the refrigerator. Sit down with me and chill."

Omari did all that he could do to take her mind off the incident. The sexy sounds of Phyllis Hyman's CD played. Omari slowly undressed Susan with his eyes. A gentle hug, kiss, and seductive slow dance led to a long night of passionate love making.

The rising morning sunlight peeked through the window and awakened Susan from her sleep. Omari, with half shut eyes, rolled over in his king size bed and glanced at the clock. It was eleven o'clock. He mumbled, I missed church." He then fell back to sleep. His syncopated snores continued to shake the walls. Susan glanced lovingly at her fiancé. Yesterday's fiasco seemed to be all but a distant memory in Susan's mind.

Susan and Omari finally woke up at two o'clock. Susan turned on the radio. Her favorite song *March* by George

Tandy, Jr. played on the radio. "You, you and me belong together. Cuz we're coming up on uncharted territories but we still march…so many obstacles facing us."

Susan strolled around the apartment in the buff until a delivery man rang the doorbell forcing her to throw on a pair of jeans and a T-shirt. Susan was elated. Her book finally arrived in the mail. It took her nearly ten years to complete the book. She was waiting for the perfect ending to the dramas in her life, but the perfect ending never came.

The voice of a well-known radio news announcer spun a round of newsworthy events on the broadcast. Susan was shocked to hear the tail end of one of the featured news stories. Susan screamed, "Hey, Omari! They are talking about us, Omari."

Omari dropped the book he was reading and ran to the small portable radio that sat on top of a pile of books in the living room.

A male with a baritone voice announced, "Omari and Susan, owners of Omari Boutique, barely escaped harm in an attempted kidnapping."

Susan sent Omari a worried look when she heard that. "Omari, I know we are always seeking interesting advertising and media relations to publicize the dealership, but this type of advertising requires an immediate public relations crisis invention strategy. We need positive publicity, Omari."

"Susan, do not fret. We are the victims who luckily escaped. God was on our side. Tomorrow, I'll place an ad in the newspaper for Omari Boutique. Then we will follow it up with a family fun night at the movies for the community, sponsored of course, by Omari Boutique."

"Susan, yesterday's event was unfortunate but it was not our fault. Life is a journey—a series of twists and turns. No one knows what today's tomorrow will be. No one holds a crystal ball, and no one knows all the answers. There's no manual or recipe for life."

Omari calmed Susan down. After they ate, Susan called a cab to take her back to her townhouse. Omari kissed her. "I'll see you tomorrow, Mrs. Thomas. I just had to try that name out on you before we walk down the aisle."

Susan's face lite up. Only her soul mate could place a childish, gleeful smile on her face.

Jazz, Blues and Rhythm

Omari Thomas was born in Pleasantville, New Jersey, a city just outside of Atlantic City. His family moved to Mount Hope, New York when he was eight years old. Atlantic City did not look like it does today. There were been no casinos. The skyline of Atlantic City had not contained ornate signs and excitement. Tons of buildings were in ill repair and in need of rehabilitation.

The boardwalk featured small stores that mostly carried T-shirts, beachwear, and souvenirs. Some of the storefronts also contained game rooms. Back in the day, these storefront game rooms housed pinball machines, basketball throws, electric ponies for the kids to ride, and a few games that required patrons to squirt water into the mouth of a clown.

"Omari loved kicking the sand on the beach and building sand castles. He hung out at the White Horse Submarine Shop, praying that a famous entertainer might walk in. The wall of the popular submarine shop was lined with signed photos of celebrities who dined there. He remembered Steel Pier Amusement Park and trolley cars.

Atlantic City blossomed into a booming casino town. New businesses were born, but gentrification came with a price. In Atlantic City, some residents were forced to leave their homes."

Many of Omari's friends realized that the real estate boom in Atlantic City would bring an influx of new jobs into the area. Some minority business owners opened businesses in Atlantic City in anticipation of the increased foot traffic brought about from high rollers and one-arm bandit fanatics.

"The African-American community, as usual, had to fight for equal employment opportunities. Omari's friends in the entertainment business became gainfully employed at the newly built hotels and casinos. Some color lines had been shattered but not all. Many hotels in Atlantic City refused to hire colored people. That's what we were called back then— colored people."

The city developed a temporary relocation plan for the Atlantic City residents whose houses were on the list to be razed but it seemed like residents who truly qualified were shafted when the wind of nepotism blew into the city. Memories couldn't be replaced. Sentimental values were hard to let go of.

The city's master plan included a plan to build affordable housing for the homeless, teachers and public service workers. First preference for affordable housing was given to city residents whose houses were taken from them by way of eminent domain. The Thomas family barely escaped—their house was located two houses away from the site where the planned razing of the houses ended. "Omari remembered his father jumping up and down with joy when he realized their house would remain unscathed."

He remembered his childhood as well.

"Omari, you go practice the piano."

Omari, a highly gifted pianist, tickled the ivory with ease. He threw his talent out the window because he did not like to practice. "Okay, Mom, after this cartoon goes off, I'll study."

His mom taught him how to play the piano in a small piano studio that she set up in the basement. As a result of receiving a lucrative contract with the local school system, Sade Thomas' music business blossomed. Private school instructions became hot when the economy spiraled downward. The first programs cut in education when the economy takes a nose-dive are usually the art and gym programs.

Omari advanced rapidly. He had a natural talent and ear for music. His sister Renee, a talented flutist, enrolled in the highly esteemed Juilliard School of Music pre-college division. Upon graduating from the program, Renee received a full academic scholarship to their undergraduate school. Renee had majored in woodwinds. Omari and Renee often performed together. In fact, Omari and Renee won many talent contests. Renee, who was two years younger than Omari, became a highly acclaimed professionally recorded performing artist. She played at some of the premier centers and theatres in New York City. Carnegie Hall, Lincoln Center, and the Apollo were just a few of the well-known concert halls where Renee performed. Her concert tours included frequent trips to Europe, Africa and the Caribbean, Haiti and Trinidad.

In addition to Omari's vocal talents, Omari also played the piano. His wonderful vocal range and perfect pitch always dazzled the audience. People flocked to performances that featured Renee and Omari.

Renee on the flute and Omari on the piano created a wonderful whisper of voices. The sound of music filled the air and resonated across the stage. Renee, a talented female contralto singer, often developed original musical compositions. Some of the poems Renee wrote were used as lyrics with her musical compositions. Renee's collaboration with a songwriter on *Push Cart King* became the number one country music tune on the country music charts.

Renee's unexpected leap into country music astonished her friends in the music industry. Renee primarily sang jazz songs. Her ability to scat often brought tears to the eyes of the audience. Audiences received a rare treat when they were able to hear the powerful gospel and jazz duets of Renee and Omari.

Harry walked on a different path. They say there's always one. In the Thomas family, it was Harry. Omari was born on Harry's thirteenth birthday. All were raised with

Christian values, but Harry enjoyed trouble. Harry bragged about scribbling in the hymnals when he was a student in a Lutheran School. Omari and Renee sung in the church choir. Harry excelled in basketball. But Renee trumped Harry's basketball skills when she spun a spin ball on her finger nail.

"I was standing right there. I could not believe it. The former Mayor of Newark, New Jersey, Corey Booker, told the Downtown Dribblers, "now spin a spin ball."

"Renee bounced that ball once and somehow put a spin on it. She slowly stuck her left index finger up and the ball fell onto her fingernail. Renee was in shock. As she felt the ball falling, she gently placed her right hand out and caught it. She looked like a pro. Renee heard people saying, a girl spun a spin ball."

Their father, James, was the proud owner of a plumbing company. James named the company after his younger son, Omari. Omari Plumbing was located right in the hub of Atlantic City. The business was very successful and well-known throughout the area. A well-known developer offered to purchase the business. Omari's father jumped on the opportunity. Monies reaped from the sale of the business paid for Omari's, Harry's and Renee's education. There was enough money to pay off the mortgage on their house.

The family relocated to Mount Hope, NY from Atlantic City when Omari was ten years old. Mount Hope is a suburb of New York City.

Omari smiled at the memories, but knowing he had a lot on his plate today, he brought himself back to the present. Omari sat at his desk. He gently opened the lid of his Toshiba laptop.

Let's see what's on today's to-do list? We need to start planning for the grand opening celebration of Omari Boutique."

"Come on what's taking so long for this program to open?" Omari clicked the mouse again. Finally, his e-mail came up. He quickly reviewed his new mail.

"Nothing needs my immediate attention."

Omari often talked out loud even though the room was empty. Omari's morning routine consisted of drinking a cup of coffee at home and eating a donut while running out the door to work. Omari realized that his habit of eating a glazed donut a day was not a good one. Sometimes he ate a breakfast sandwich at Dunkin Donuts on his way to work was a given.

Omari dressed in fashionable casual attire this morning—a button-down white shirt with a bright-colored tie and black cotton pants. He kept a black designer suit in his large private office at Omari Boutique for unexpected business meetings.

Omari checked his voicemail for messages.

"Hello, Mr. Thomas, this is Officer Manley. Please call us as soon as possible."

Omari immediately phoned the police station. "Hello, Officer Manley, this is Omari Thomas. How can I help you?

"Omari, we need to meet with you as soon as possible. Can you possibly come into the office tomorrow morning at ten o'clock?"

"Sure, I'll be there. In fact, if you want me to come now, I can come."

"Actually noon works better for me, Omari."

"Okay, that works for me. I'll see you in a few hours, Officer Manley."

Omari grabbed his laptop and the laptop carrier. He placed his laptop in the back of the car, turned on the ignition, and drove to the boutique.

Upon entering the boutique, Omari immediately noticed that Emeka Adewale, an award winning Nigerian painter and the Moises Suirel limited edition *Red Storm* oil painting were slightly tilted to the side. Omari adjusted the paintings, sat at his desk and read the newspaper. The first round of fresh hazel nut coffee was brewed. Omari liked his coffee light and sweet. One cup of coffee in the morning just was not enough.

He completed his bookkeeping tasks and left the office around 11:00 a.m. so that he could arrive at the fifth precinct on time for his noon appointment.

Officer Manley, who appeared to be in his early fifties, escorted Omari into a private room.

Manley said, "Omari, we were able to locate the alleged representatives from the network. The case is airtight. One of the survivors of the crime is going to be charged as a felon. The men who posed as representatives of the television station intended to do a photo shoot of the gallery so that they could successfully steal the art. They needed to film the inside of the property so that they knew the exact locations of all paintings. They observed the location of all cameras in the store. The theft had to occur within the same week to ensure that most of the art pieces were located in the same places on the wall. However, once they received a text message that the kidnapping attempt failed, they scrubbed the plan and disconnected their phone service."

"That's interesting, Officer Manley. As you know, Susan and I never met the men."

"They cased your boutique. They noticed that you were in the process of featuring the original artwork of Moises Suirel and a relatively unknown Nigerian artist Emeka Adewele. They were savvy. They needed to know the exact location of all paintings. The thieves quickly observed the Omari Boutique security system and scanned the systems hardware into a computerized disc system so that they could disarm the system remotely. Disarming the system immediately disengages the security system. Once triggered, no alert is sent to the police and fire station."

Officer Manley advised Omari that WCDQ intended to prosecute these two characters to the fullest extent of the law. They were charged with impersonation.

These clowns are known in the area and have successfully stolen art from a number of museums and art galleries.

"Since Jill is the one who saw the men, we need to talk to her. When will Jill be in the store?"

"She should be in the store at 1:00 p.m."

"Can you have Jill come into the station as soon as possible?"

"Sure, I'll arrange for transportation to the police station."

"I need her to identify the men."

When the first plan failed, the not-so-dynamic duo resorted to another plan. Pedro Nimo, under intense grilling, finally admitted that the team was much larger than the police knew.

"Officer Manley, this boutique actually began as an online business. When our sales skyrocketed, I decided to find a commercial storefront property so that the artwork could be featured in a small but intimate jazz spot. We can promote and develop intimate after work events so that people can network and perform."

"You truly do not realize the amount of exposure the boutique has garnered over the years—our online sales are brisk."

Omari returned to the store with a fresh bouquet of exotic flowers. He snuck up behind Susan. Susan felt the heat of warm breath beating upon her neck and turned around.

"Omari, don't do that! You nearly scared the living daylights out of me, Omari."

Omari presented the beautiful arrangement of flowers to Susan. Omari used to accompany his father to his father's sister's floral shop, Flowers by Emily. Susan loved the fresh scent of flowers.

"Susan, where's Jill?" asked Omari.

"She's in the back room replenishing stock for the show-room. I'll go get her." Omari conducted an impromptu meeting to discuss the current investigation. Once Jill heard the full details of the case, she was shocked.

What, you got to be kidding! Said Jill.

"Since you were the only person to see the two men, the police want to talk to you."

"You will need to identify the suspect. I'll give you money for the cab ride. They want you to report to the police station immediately. Ask for Officer Abbott when you arrive. He is expecting you. The suspects are in jail."

"Of course, Omari, you know I got your back."

Omari gave Jill the cab fare. He thanked her for her cooperation and told her to take the rest of the day off.

"Not a problem," said Jill. She quickly departed from the store. Jill was lucky. She spotted a cab driving down the block and hailed it. Sometimes cabs passed by minorities. Omari told Jill that he received complaints from a number of their customers about cabs passing them by. Jill reported the incidents to the Newark Police Department Taxi and Limousine Commission.

A few of the incidents occurred right in front of the boutique. A few months ago, Susan threatened to stage a protest in front of the Newark Police Department Taxi and Limousine Commission when a number of high profile customers complained that taxis were passing them by.

Just as she was about to step her foot into the cab, Omari ran out the store and shouted, "Jill, don't forget to ask for Officer Abbott."

Jill instructed the driver of the cab to drive her to the fifth precinct. She read a few pages of Susan's recently released novel during the ride. Officer Abbott escorted Jill into a starkly lit room. Abbott asked her to give a full account of what occurred. Jill described the inaudible entrance of the men.

"They quietly observed the art pieces displayed on the gallery walls. "Who is they, Jill," asked Officer Abbott. "The men from WQCD. I approached them. At one point, I noticed they separated, but that did not seem unusual to me."

"Did they go into the café?"

"I don't know. The store was unusually busy that day. I divided my attention between front desk duties and docent activities. The phones started ringing. In fact, shortly after receiving a phone call from Omari, it seemed like the switchboard was flooded with calls. One of the men approached me. He identified himself as Mr. Lynton. Lynton wanted me to give his business card to the owner of the boutique because his network was in the midst of developing a series on art boutiques. The concept of art boutique and cafes suddenly has become a hot topic."

"I called Omari and informed him about the men's desire to film the store for a featured story on WQCD."

"Thanks, Jill, I have arranged a line up—follow me," said Officer Abbott. "You'll be behind a mirrored window. You can see them, but they will not be able to see you. That way you are protected."

A line of men dressed in orange prison uniforms walked into the room. The men quickly turned toward the protective window.

Jill immediately said, "That's them—suspect number 3 and 7."

"Suspects number 3 and 7 positively identified. Book them," said Officer Abbott.

The police thanked Jill. Jill departed from the station. Being the workaholic that she was, Jill returned to the store. Turned out, she made the right decision. The store was busy. Omari was surprised to see her standing in the entry-way. He graciously thanked her for cooperating.

Jill engaged in friendly conversation with the patrons. Jill, a natural born salesperson, was well skilled in stimulating interesting conversation. Patrons enjoyed the personal attention they received at the boutique. Jill discussed their upcoming Grand Opening ceremony with the customers. The event would feature a well-known personality. Jill added, "I promise you, this event is going be hot."

It was an unusually lucrative day for the boutique. By the end of the day, a number of sales were processed. The lovely art pieces that Omari and Susan purchased in Philadelphia were sold.

Omari and Jill rode home together. Susan returned to her upscale townhouse in Maplewood. Susan often threw lavish parties. Bloom, a very spoiled cream colored standard poodle puppy greeted Susan at the door with a loud happy bark. Susan's first task was to open the mail. One envelope immediately caught her eye. She gingerly opened the letter. A loud scream echoed through her home.

I won the literary contest!" She checked the two round-trip tickets to Chicago in the envelope. Susan kissed the first-class tickets and placed them on her desk for safe keeping. Susan's hard work finally paid off. In her spare time, she would have spent many hours in front of the computer, typing creative proses, designing computer art and writing poetry.

A meal of green pea soup with ham was carefully placed on the stove. Her unfinished art project seemed to call out her name. Susan glued a photo of a mansion on the canvas. Art became her therapy and calling. "*The Calling*—I think I'll name this piece *The Calling*."

Susan's enrollment in a continuing education class for graphic arts proved to be valuable. She developed an independent website for her highly successful creative website design company. The company was well established before she met Omari. The award winning Omari Boutique website design generated increased sales and customers.

Just as she placed the finishing touches on her multi-media art design the phone rang.

"Hello, my dear, what's up," said Omari in his baritone voice.

"I won, I won the contest. Remember, I submitted an article to the magazine. Are you coming with me to the awards ceremony? The ceremony will be held in May in the windy city of Chicago—it's the big one. We have to be dressed to the nines. I already called Africa, and they are going to design an African dress for me to wear to the occasion."

"I'll get my tuxedo out of the cleaners and buy a new pair of shoes."

"Omari you are too much. You know you have a closet full of shoes. You said you would buy a new pair of shoes every day for a month and wear a new pair of shoes every day, once you met your 'soul mate.' Well, you finally met me! I think you better get to buying. Just make sure you don't wear those squeaky shoes again."

"Boy did those shoes squeak."

"Make sure the new shoes don't screech like the ones you wore when you got your award."

Omari laughed. He knew that his shoes screeched like a lost mouse in a maze. "There is nothing like the sound of a pair of screeching shoes. I threw those shoes away. Even when you try to quiet them by walking slowly—it just does not work." Susan hollered. She too experienced the embarrassment of buying a cheap pair of shoes—the sound of the squeaking woke up the entire room.

"Sleep tight Susan, my love, my Queen and reason for living." Omari quietly blew a kiss into Susan's ear and gently hung up the phone.

In My Waking Hours

THE SOUND OF MUSIC FROM her digital alarm clock awakened Susan from her somber sleep. "I am every woman—it's all in me."

"Okay, Chaka, I got the message."

Susan turned over and snapped the snooze button on the alarm clock. She quickly turned back on her side for another ten minutes of sleep. Again, the loud sounds from the radio alarm clock reverberated in her sleep.

The sudden sound of the male newscaster's voice, announcing the customary list of murders that occurred in the city became all too familiar."

"Unarmed teenager shot in the back by a cop was found to be unarmed.

"Fifty-one shots rang out in the night. A young dashing black man about to marry his children's mother never made it to the wedding. Instead he was met with a hail of bullets while leaving his bachelor party."

I know it must be about 6:25 a.m., thought Susan as she slowly rose up from her bed. *That's about the time the news comes on. If only I could just get five more minutes of sleep. The daily inspirational message is over. It's time for me to rise and shine.*

Susan finally succumbed to the call of the alarm clock. She wiped the sleep from her eyes and stumbled down the hallway to her bathroom. She showered and quickly brushed her teeth. Susan grabbed her two-piece black pantsuit and multicolored button down shirt from the closet. A little makeup covered the blemishes on her face. Taupe blush and cafe taupe lipstick made her look fabulous. She quickly stuck her black high-heeled pumps on her feet, poured her coffee into the travel coffee mug and dashed out the door. "Bloom will you move out the way, move! Can't you see, Bloom, I got no time to give you much love this morning."

Bloom stood in front of the door as if to say, "You are not leaving until you pat me on the head and cuddle me." He went as far as standing on his hind legs with his front paws placed lightly on Susan's lower leg. Susan succumbed to the wants of her pompous puppy. Bloom was only six weeks old but he was already very demanding. Bloom loved affection. Just prior to leaving the house Susan placed Bloom in his lavish Poop-House designer cage that was built like a castle. Sometimes Susan envied her dog's lifestyle. One morning she loudly voiced to Omari, "If I could just live the life of a pampered puppy than I would not have to fight the morning traffic."

Susan stepped out the door. A ton of residents gathered in the hallway. Looks of horror and anguish painted were on their faces, a sign that something awful occurred. They seemed alarmed. She eased her way through the crowd. In the not-too-far distance, Susan observed police cars on the block with their flashing red lights and the raucous sound of sirens piercing through the early morning daylight. She knew something bad happened. As Susan approached the scene, it was clear that there was a car accident.

Susan gasped at the sight of a man lying still on a gurney. Smoke lingered in the air. The mangled white car surrounded by firemen with hoses formed a line in the street.

"Oh my god!"

Residents of the normally quiet community quietly watched and cried when all realized that the fresh smell of death penetrated the air.

"Are you all right, lady?"

Susan blurted out a tearful "Yes. I recognize the car and..."

Paramedics slowly lifted the white sheet over her neighbor's face. Tears streamed down Susan's face. The sound of a beep emanating from her cell phone abruptly awakened her from her sorrow. Susan checked the text message: "Please call."

Susan phoned the number and apologized to Omari. Susan sobbed wildly on the phone. In a choked voice she was finally able to whisper, "That's my neighbor. You met my neighbor, George. He just got killed in a car accident. I will arrive as soon as possible. The entry way is blocked. The police closed off the entrance to the complex."

"Okay, honey, take your time. I know you are upset. I can hear it in your voice."

Susan was one and a half hours late for work. She was visibly shaken.

"Omari that guy was friendly. He never caused any problems in the complex. He has two English Terrier dogs named Lucky and Ninja. I wonder if anyone saved them, Omari. Whenever I needed help, he willingly helped. I attended a few cocktail parties at his home."

"Mr. O'Shea, that was his name, he always had an interesting crowd of people at his parties. He referred a number of clients to the boutique. He purchased a number of art pieces from the Omari Boutique and proudly displayed the art on his walls."

"It was his time, Susan. No one knows the time that death will come knocking at our door."

Shortly after Susan's arrival her cousin Donald entered the store. Donald, a tall dashing man of strong structure and flawless caramel colored skin often attracted the stares of women.

Donald, a highly paid commissioned import/export specialist, developed Omari Boutique's international import/export division. This division purchased, sold and imported art pieces from Africa as well as a number of Caribbean islands.

"Hey cuz, said Donald." Susan kissed Donald lightly on the cheek.

"What orders do you have today Susan?"

"We have a number of personal requests from our customers. One of the items needs to be delivered within a week." Susan sat down at her desk, gathered the orders together and reviewed the transaction with Donald. "So what is new, Susan, asked Donald?"

"Not much, Donald. Oh, I did I tell you I won an award."

"Congratulations, what kind of award did you win?

"A literary contest. My short story won first prize."

"Omari and I are flying to Chicago. That's where the awards ceremony will be held."

"I am elated, Susan. Is there any way that I can attend the award ceremony?" "I don't know Donald, but I'll inquire." "Thanks cuz. Dreams fulfilled come around once in a lifetime sometimes," said Donald.

He slowly bent over and planted a congratulatory kiss on Susan's cheek. "How about I take you out to lunch so that we can celebrate your victory?"

"Sounds like a plan to me, Donald."

Donald said, "Fine."

"I am free on Friday, Susan."

"That will work for me too, Donald. I'll call you later. I have another appointment to attend to."

Donald stood up and walked toward the door. Donald waved good-bye to Omari.

Jill busied herself in the store by dusting off the soapstone statue, Benin Mask and pictures. She pretended not to notice this gorgeous hunk of a man who was heading for the door of the boutique. She proceeded to the computer to search for incoming orders. Processing the orders in their automated system was easy but somewhat time consuming.

"Hey, Omari, I don't mean to interfere with your business but this computer system is cumbersome. I am sure they have a better computer program than this."

"Tell you what Jill, I want you to research this and return with a list of alternative programs. I just might consider changing the program."

"Okay, Omari." "Give me three weeks to research this."

"Oh I hear the phone ringing, Omari, I'll get it."

"Omari Boutique, Jill speaking. How may I help you?"

There was a long, pregnant pause of silence on the other end of the line.

"Hello?" Jill heard the sudden sound of a click."

Jill did not think much about the call until she received another mysterious call later that evening. Little did Jill know that the silence represented a mystery that would slowly unfold over time.

Afrolena resided in a three-bedroom apartment with her mother, son, and daughter in the historic Forest Hills area of Newark, New Jersey.

"Where's Rose?" asked Jill. Jill knew Rose was hiding; she loved to play hide-and-seek.

"Hi, Mom," said Rose. Rose ran towards her mother and kissed her. Rose, a cute, petite five-year-old girl with long braids and a wide smile, showed her mother the artwork she completed at school.

Rose's pleasant personality, quick wit and humor charmed many. Her ten-year-old brother, Eric, loved to read. He was a math whiz. He maintained an A average in all his classes. Eric, a bookworm, sometimes had to be pulled up for air. He needed constant intellectual stimulation.

"Where's my man Eric?" said Jill.

"I'm here, Ma. I am in the den researching a project for school." Eric pretended to be nonplussed to his mother's presence.

"Come give your mother some sugar."

He ran from his chair with a paper in his hand. He immediately jumped onto his mother's lap and kissed her. "See, Ma, I got an A on my math quiz." Eric hugged and planted a kiss on her cheek.

"That's great, Eric. I'm going to hang this on the refrigerator."

Rose danced in the background to the music that emanated from the stereo.

"I see the dance lessons I paid for are paying off."

Rose grabbed a floppy hat and feathers from her toy chest.

"Hold on, honey. I just have to take a picture of this to send to your father." Jill grabbed her 35mm digital camera and snapped a series of shots.

Rose, a natural-born ham, posed for the camera with her brother, who was known to be camera shy. She loved every minute of this impromptu photo shoot. Jill enjoyed laughing with her children.

"When's Daddy coming home?" asked Eric.

"I hope he comes home soon, Eric. I miss him too."

Jill took her customary nap until a nightmare interrupted her sleep. Only vivid dreams remained in Jill's memory. This dream was so vivid that it frightened her. Sand flowing through the cracks into a room blocked the exit door and flowed to Jill's neckline. She continued to walk through an aisle. A man followed her. Jill realized the door was being covered by the sand and retreated, but it was too late. A sudden avalanche of sand drifted swiftly through the room. When the sands stopped flowing, Jill turned toward the man shouting, "Where are the children?"

The man responded, "They are safe. They are back there."

She woke up with a gasp.

Everyone stood in a moving wave of dry sand.

She jumped out of the bed and ran to her children's room. They were not there.

"Where are my babies?"

Jill ran from the children's room into the living room.

"Eric, Rose!" shouted Jill.

The children responded in unison, "Yes, Mom."

Jill did not want to alarm the children, so she played it off. "How about we go to the park?"

"Yeah," screamed the children.

The Branch Brook Park playground, located two blocks away from their home, became a second home for the children. The cherry blossom trees are in full bloom in April. Eric swung on the swings and Rose slid down the slide while Jill quietly read Susan's hot new novel, *I'll Finish This Before I Die,* a novel that was destined for the silver screen.

As the sun began to set, she beckoned to the children. "Eric and Rose, it's time to go home.

The area was relatively safe. Drug dealers and gangs had not yet infested the area. The Forest Hill area of Newark featured beautiful turn-of-the-century mansions and mini-mansions. These homes are small compared to the houses that the rich and famous occupy today.

Jill loved to take the children to the annual Lincoln Park Music Festival. House music was born in the Brick City. The annual festival is held in Lincoln Park. Men playing cards, dominoes and vendors selling books, clothes, and incense enhanced the distinct bohemian flavor to the area during the festival.

Jill held the hands of both her children as they walked peacefully down Board Street. On occasion, strangers approached Jill on the street, wanting to take photos of her children.

Jill and the children gleefully sang together as they strolled down the cement streets. Jill suddenly stopped singing when she felt someone grab her around her waist. Although startled, this grab carried a familiar feel. Jill slowly turned around and screamed when she realized that Leon was holding her around the waist.

The children screamed, "Daddy."

"Surprise, the job assignment overseas did not last as long as the government anticipated."

The children looked on as their parents embraced and kissed each other. Eric and Rose looked at each other clapped hands and cheered.

"Yuck!" screamed Eric. Please stop the osculation."

"What." screamed Leon. Who taught Eric that word?

"I tried to tell you Leon, Eric is a genius."

Leon laughed—osculation? Excuse me. "Eric, we will stop the kissing in our time not your time."

Leon Sullivan, an interracial man with chiseled cheeks and green eyes graduated from Harvard Law School with high honors. Leon's green eyes were gifted to him from his Irish mother. She was born in the South. Leon's father was born in Jamaica. He worked as an attorney at a prestigious law firm, but he was also in the army reserves.

When troops were sent to the Middle East, Leon was called for active duty. His initial orders indicated that he would serve for a minimum of one year.

Leon was upset. He prayed for a safe return home. Prior to leaving, he made provisions for his family. He moved them out of their two-bedroom apartment. He did not feel comfortable leaving them there alone. He felt it was best for them to move into his mother-in-law's house. Ironically, this move would place them right across the street from

Omari. Leon knew that Omari would keep a mindful eye on his family.

Leon grew up in Newark's South Ward district. Leon excelled in sports during his high school years. He was the star quarterback for Newark's Central High School. Leon turned down a million-dollar football contract because he wanted to be a corporate lawyer.

Leon never left the Newark area until he moved to Waltham, Massachusetts to attend Brandeis University. He received a full academic sports scholarship to Brandeis University. He breezed through school. At the age of four, Leon knew what he wanted to be when he grew up. In fact, he told his grandmother, "I'm going to be a lawyer when I grow up." He never changed his mind. He turned down a lucrative contract with the Washington Redskins.

Leon was accepted into the prestigious Harvard Law School. Harvard required mandatory enrollment in Harvard's legal pro bono clinical practice program. The program provided him with the tools that he needed to succeed. A minority owned law firm noticed his strong skills. Prior to his graduation, they offered him a position in their entertainment law division. His decision to focus his attention on business law paid off. He stayed at the prestigious minority law firm until he was offered a partnership at Watson, White, and Berger.

After three long years of sleepless nights and a million cups of coffee, Leon graduated from Harvard with high honors. He was the valedictorian and graduation speaker.

Leon proudly stepped to the podium. A round of applause filled the stadium.

"Students, parents, esteemed faculty and board members we welcome you. Allow me to be the first student to congratulate our class's victory!"

A loud cheer from the audience, faculty and graduates roared into the heavens. Jill eased her way through the crowd so that she could hand her fiancee a rose bouquet.

Leon met Jill at a dance that was held at Brandeis University. Jill majored in education and minored in art at Brandeis University. Leon majored in the pre-law business degree program and was enrolled in ROTC.

Brandeis' minority enrollment was relatively small. Under the direction of the minority recruiter, a strong black student union was formed. The BSU developed a number of events and social responsibility programs. The black student union also sponsored campus parties.

Leon spotted Jill standing in the corner in the darkened room that was converted from a dining hall to a ballroom for the party. He was instantly taken by her beauty. Her smile beamed across the room. Leon walked slowly towards her. Their first dance led to a life-long relationship.

Leon often boasted to his friends about his love for Jill. "Jill is the one I would lay my life down for. No storm will toss us overboard."

Three months after Leon's graduation from Harvard Law School, Jill and Leon married in a small wedding ceremony held on the campus of Harvard.

"With this ring I thee wed." Leon quietly whispered in Jill's ear, "I promise to buy you a house one day."

Two years later, Leon's promise to purchase a home became a reality.

The closing was scheduled for Valentine Day. There were no problems at the closing table. Even the lawyers commented that unlike some closing, this closing went off without a hitch.

The bank attorney congratulated Omari. "You are now the proud owner of this house. Here's the keys to your house."

"Thank you! I have not told my wife yet."

Leon decided to treat his wife to an elaborate Valentine's Day dinner date and night of passionate lovemaking at a luxury hotel. Prior to arriving at the Plaza hotel they attended a gospel concert and ate dinner at the Mansion, a trendy upscale restaurant that features the culinary talents of world- renowned Chef Eric Harford.

A side excursion to Bloomingdale's included a romp through the intimate wear department. Leon purchased a nice negligee for his wife. Leon picked out a red baby doll negligee with matching thong panties. Jill adored her husband's selection.

They gleefully walked hand-in-hand to the perfume counter. The sales associate dressed in all black informed the amorous couple. "You are going to love this scent." She quickly sprayed the perfume on Jill's wrist.

"There's a special on this perfume."

Jill sniffed her wrist. "Oh, I love it" Jill planted a kiss on Leon's cheek. The salesperson wrapped up the perfume but did not request money.

"Leon, we are going to be arrested. You better pay for that."

"She gave it to us."

"She might lose her job."

Leon ushered Jill to the escalator. Leon pointed out the sheer, ethereal banner that read "In the Wind by Omari, Scents for You and Yours," blowing gently. The banner could not be ignored. It was perfectly located between the escalators.

Jill screamed, "Oh my god! Omari hid the fact that he extended the brand to include a new perfume line." "Look inside the bag, Jill."

The outside of the neatly wrapped gift box contained a card that read," To Jill and Leon, Thank you! We hope that you enjoy our new line of perfume—Much love, Omari."

Jill phoned Omari immediately. The excitement in her voice could not be contained. Thank you, Omari for the special gift. This perfume is superb."

Omari knew about the surprise. He planned it with Leon. Omari laughed. "I hope you two enjoy your night out on the town."

They arrived at the luxury condo suites located in midtown, where a fabulous three-bedroom penthouse suite awaited their arrival.

Immediately upon opening the door, the fresh scents of flowers emanated. The suite was warmly decorated. The Jacuzzi-style bathtub was lined with oils, bath beads, and candles. The living room table was set. Leon whispered softly in her ear, "open the box."

Jill opened the box and found a key inside. "What's this key to Leon?"

"This is the key to our brownstone. Happy Valentine's Day!" Jill screamed.

Omari found a fabulously wide and renovated brownstone in the Clinton Hill section of Brooklyn. The Hill is surrounded by Prospect Park, Crown Heights, Bedford Stuyvesant, Prospect Heights, Fort Greene, and Williamsburg. Brooklyn is a mecca and a fertile ground for African-American artists. It is a prime location to promote and cultivate the arts for black arts and culture.

"There's a rental unit in the basement that can be occupied by your mother. You know I would not exclude your mother."

"Omari decided to open a second Omari Boutique in Brooklyn. He wants you to run it Jill. I'm going to provide the financial backing for the boutique. Five years later we anticipate building a store in Radioland. Radioland is located in Richmond, VA. Richmond out beats NY in terms of the number of minority programming radio stations. Plus there are a number of colleges in the Tri-City area. Richmond's First Friday Art Walks are popular."

Jill's face brightened like a well-lit Christmas tree.

"Wow, I am honored!"

"Baby you are the best, Leon. I love you." Jill planted a long kiss on Leon's lascivious lips.

By February 20th all of their items were placed on a moving truck and moved to Brooklyn, New York.

A neighbor sat at the window and watched the moving men unload their items from the truck.

Jill worked as a teacher in the Newark School system, but her career in education was interrupted when she became pregnant with Eric. She never returned to teaching. Instead, she became a full-time housewife and mother. By the time their youngest child was born, Leon had established a prominent name in law. He was featured in *Ebony* magazine and in trade magazines. Leon specialized in corporate law at Watson, White, and Berger.

Leon received many offers from outside law firms while employed at Watson, but he decided not to leave the firm when they offered him a limited partnership in the company.

Shortly after moving to Brooklyn, Leon received orders from the army to report for active duty. Within a week he would be deployed to the battlefields in the Middle East.

Leon and Jill returned home to find their children sitting in front of the plasma-screen television, laughing. Their eyes were stuck on the screen as they watched the Mr. Giggle's Show, a cartoon for children that aired on Saturday mornings.

Rose excitedly asked her mom and dad, "What are we doing today?"

They always looked forward to their Saturday outings.

"We have a big surprise for you and Eric."

"You'll see, son," said Leon to Eric.

"See what?" said Eric.

"It's a secret. That is why it is a surprise. Hurry up. Get dressed. The show begins at 2:00 p.m."

"What show, Dad?"

"I told you, it's a surprise. Is Grandma up?"

Grandma yelled from the back room, "Yes, I am up, Leon."

Jill yelled, "Hurry up. Get dressed. I can't wait to show you."

"Show me what?"

Jill shouted, "I told you—it's a surprise."

Everyone jumped into the luxurious, taupe colored Mercedes Benz. Jill placed the DVD in the dashboard so that the children and her mother could watch the movie that she purchased for them the other night. They never did watch the movie together that night. Leon pulled onto a beautiful, tree lined street and parked the car outside of a brownstone. Eric, in a loud, high-pitched voice, said, "We have never been here before."

Leon screamed, "Surprise!

This is our new address. I found the house online and contacted a close friend of mine who is a real estate broker from overseas. Prior to returning home, I signed the contracts, and we were able to set up a closing overseas. The engineer report returned with a rating of four stars out of a possible five stars. No major repairs were needed, the CO for the kitchen and the basement were complete. It was an easy deal to close."

Everyone ran to the front stairs. Even Grandma Louise, who sometimes walked with a limp, managed to run today. Eric and Rose laughed at the sight of their grandmother tossing down her crane. She ran up the stairs. "You can run, Grandma Louise!" shouted Rose.

"Ohhh I'm going to tell… you been faking it, grandma."

"They say fake it till you can make it."

They broke out into a chorus of "Go Grandma Go."

Rose developed the song, and Eric quickly joined in.

Leon opened the door.

Eric and Rose screamed, "Wow."

Leon insisted on carrying Jill over the threshold.

"Leon you are crazy; we are not newlyweds," responded Jill. Both burst into laughter.

Beautiful hardwood floors, wide windows, and plenty of sunlight abound in this brownstone. The kitchen contains a center island, and the counter tops are covered with speckled brown and black granite. The solid wood kitchen cabinets, contain silver handles stand out. The extraordinary three-bedroom apartment, contained top-of-the-line modern features, including a robust living room with wood-burning fireplace, a powder room, dining room and eat-in kitchen with center island. A wide stairway to the second floor faces the exposed brick walls on the side wall of the duplex apartment. The second floor's tremendous master bedroom with oversized tub, separate stall shower and working fireplace created a warm and romantic feel.

The kids ran around the apartment.

"This is my room proclaimed Eric." "I'm bigger than you, so I get the larger room."

Rose pouted, held her head down, and wrapped her arms around her waist.

Jill and Leon quietly laughed. Leon said, "They will get over it. Eric picked the room I actually choose for him."

The backyard is sizable for a brownstone yard. Eric said," mommy when we move can we take the rose brush with us."

"Eric honey, I think we will have to leave the rose bush behind, but we can plant a new rose bush and watch it grow."

Grandma walked to the basement apartment. She immediately noticed there is a separate entry to her apartment that can be entered into from the front of the house. Grandma's journey to her private apartment consisted of walking down two steps to the entry door of the apartment. "This apartment is tremendous. "I love the size of these bedrooms and there's plenty of closet space. This living room is grand. My baby grand piano will fit perfectly in the corner. Thank you, Jesus for our blessing," shouted Grandma Louise.

A separate area for the washer and dryer was neatly tucked away in a closet in each apartment. The roof top housed a neatly manicured garden. This stunning brownstone featured a brown-speckled granite hand rail and is located in a low-crime area. The block also featured a number of historic landmarks. Some of the brownstones will be featured on a brownstone walking tour in the fall.

Leon advised Jill that this new home is located just a few blocks away from the train stop. "Jill, you can take the train to the new store. The store will open in May. The new store is located near the subway stop and a popular soul food restaurant."

Everyone loved the house. Leon dragged them out the house so that they would arrive on time for the two o'clock showing of the live interactive art exhibit of *Mr. Giggles*. Leon gathered his family together and drove to the Brooklyn Museum. Leon shouted, "Its *Mr. Giggles* time." He loved the *Mr. Giggles* show.

"Yeah! Yeah!" screamed Eric and Rose. They ran from the car to the admissions gate.

Jill, Leon, and Louise cracked up.

Monday morning quickly arrived. Being that it was a holiday weekend, Jill did not have to report to work on Friday or Saturday. Omari hired another person to work in the boutique on a per-diem basis. Wednesday's resume stood out from the rest. She attended a school that specialized in art management. Omari positioned himself for change. Wednesday worked when Jill was not on the schedule. Unknown to Wednesday, in time she would replace Jill at their Newark based store.

Jill prepared a breakfast of French toast and bacon. The cell phone rang.

"Hello," said Jill.

Dead silence resonated in her ear.

Jill repeated, "Hello?"

There was no answer. Within the past two weeks Jill received a number ominous phone calls.

Jill thought, *Mmm I wonder if these calls might be tied to the Omari Boutique case.*

Jill neglected to tell Leon about the case. Leon entered the kitchen in his pajamas and slippers. Sleep was still in his eyes. He was not scheduled to return to the law firm until the end of the month.

"Honey, sit down. I need to tell you about these strange phone calls I have recently received." Jill explained the Omari Boutique incident to Leon.

Jill said, "there was an art theft investigation going on at the gallery. Because of the investigation, the police requested that I provide information about two mysterious men who showed up at the boutique disguised as representatives from a television station. Ever since than there have been a series of strange phone calls to the boutique and personal cell phone."

Suddenly the phone rang. The sound of footsteps in the back ground could be heard. Than there was a sudden click.

"Hello, hello," said Jill—

The sound of silence and a sudden click met her ear.

Leon decided to alert the police about these troublesome phone calls. Jill had nothing to hide, and she just wanted the haunting calls to stop.

Jill drove with the children to Brooklyn. A well-known children's theatrical agency scheduled a talent search for aspiring child performers. Jill decided to attend the talent search. Rose was always creative.

Traffic was fairly light. A speeding car nearly clipped their car as it weaved in and out of traffic. Jill set the navigation to a Greenwich Village location and placed a gospel CD into the player. Jill sang along with the song "I'll Fly Away." Little did she know that in time she would become known for her rendition of this celebratory funeral song.

Jill called Leon from her high-tech car.

"Hi dear. I forgot to turn the stove off, Leon."

"I got it. Shortly after you left I noticed the red light on the stove.

"Leon some of my best thoughts occur in the car. I was just thinking about the choir I used to sing in. I'm going to enter the choir in the *Sunday Best* open auditions."

Leon replied, "To the best of my knowledge *Sunday Best* focuses on soloist."

"What made you think about nominating the choir to sing on a television show, Jill?"

"I don't know Leon, it must have been the Holy Spirit."

"That *Change* choir was interesting but I noticed that a few members in the choir tried to out sing other members of the choir."

"I am sure Dr. Milton Davis will teach the choir how to breathe and not holler. They need to blend their sounds. After the musical director trains the choir they might even get a record contract with the *Camdon* record label."

Camdon Records specializes in gospel music. *Camdon* records, promotes and trains new gospel artists on the art of the business, interviewing skills, and explains contractual agreements. This company acts as a spring board to other record companies."

Jill called Sharpton. "Hi Sharpton this is Jill. I used to sing in the *Change* choir.

"Jill, I remember you they placed you right in front of me. You were the strong fist thrower."

"Yep, that's me. I have decided to nominate the *Change* choir for the Next One Up television show. That show will focus on choirs. It's suppose to premiere in the Fall. They looked great in their black jeans, black tee shirt and sneakers. I hope they wear that outfit."

"That sounds good, go on and nominate the choir. We can discuss the details later on, Jill. I got to go I'm running for my flight to DC. I'll call you from DC. I'm going to an art show and a conference on gun violence. Tell your husband I said hello."

Jill hung up the phone. She arrived at her destination. The lot was full.

After filling out the necessary paperwork, Rose tried out for a role in an upcoming off-Broadway play. The casting director immediately picked Rose to perform the lead role in *"Two Cats and a Bunk Bed,"* an original play written by a local playwright.

Jill had no intentions of placing Eric in the auditions, but one of the casting agents suggested that he audition. "Jill, we encourage family unity. That's why we want Eric to audition."

"Eric is shy," responded Jill. He's a bookworm."

The casting agent replied, "Don't worry. We specialize in breaking children out of shyness. He is very handsome. I can see the girls will trip over their feet chasing after him when he gets old. He can be an extra. This might just help him to overcome some of his shyness."

"I have the perfect role for him. He'll love it. I recall you mentioning that Eric loves to read. I need someone to dust and return the books back onto the book shelves in the library. Then he can quietly sit down and act like he is reading a book."

Jill laughed. "Pretend? You don't know my son. He'll read the book on the stage. I swear, one day he is going to be an award-winning journalist or novelist. Okay, sign Eric up."

Jill, Eric, and Rose's performance ignited the judged. The children were chosen to perform in the play. Eric shouted, Yes! I get to read the books on stage! Let's celebrate Mommy!"

"Sounds like a plan to me, Eric. There's a whimsical children's play at the Brooklyn Museum, son. We have enough time to get there on time for the five o'clock show. You might even pick up some tips on acting." Eric and Rose laughed and than ran to the car.

Upon entering the museum, Jill observed a large crowd of children and parents enthralled in a live puppet show in the children's pavilion. The steady sound of footsteps resonated behind her. Slowly the sound of hundreds of footsteps dissipated into a duet of footsteps. She quickly observed a tall grimy-looking white male walking behind her. She grabbed hold of her children's hands and quickly escaped into another hallway. Jill watched the man walk past in the hallway. He pulled out his cell phone, but they were too far behind him to hear his conversation. Jill quickly exited the exhibit with her children and drove toward their home.

"Mom, Mom," said Eric, "can we stop for pizza? Little Joe's has the best pizza in town. See, it's right there."

Jill, Eric and Rose entered Little Joe's Pizza Shop. They waited twenty minutes for a table. "What do you want to order?" Rose ordered the chicken lasagna pizza. Eric ordered the house specialty pizza and Jill ordered a plain slice of pizza. They were regular customers at Little Joe's.

Eric noticed a toy store across the street from the pizza shop. "That's new, a toy store," said Eric as he pointed to the store.

"We'll go to the toy store after you finish eating."

"Yep," said Eric.

The kids gobbled down their food and drink. Eric headed straight to the computer aisle. Rose wanted a new doll. The ride back home was peaceful and uneventful.

Eric anxiously waited for his mother to install the new computer game on his all-in-one desktop computer. Eric's computer contained a number educational game programs and videos. The kids spent the bulk of the evening playing with their new toys. Jill sent them to bed around eight o'clock. She began the tedious task of packing up items for the move.

Just prior to Jill settling down in her bed, she looked out the window. A car was parked outside her door. There appeared to be a man inside the car, and the lights were turned off. He lingered there for far too long.

Jill quickly closed the curtain and turned the lights off. Leon arrived home late that night. He attended a company-sponsored fundraising event at Citi Field. A few of his classmates also attended the game.

Jill had fallen asleep but woke up when Leon gently kissed her on the cheek. In a slurred groggy voice, Jill asked Leon who won the game.

Leon said, The Mets, two to one." She immediately rolled over and fell back to sleep.

Jill was awakened by the sounds of the tweeting birds. While rubbing the sleep from her eyes and yawning, Jill caught a glimpse of the ominous black car still parked front of her door. Jill could see the white smoke rings coming from the tailpipe. She was able to see the inside of the car. The driver's side door was wide open.

Jill immediately shook her husband from his sleep and summoned him to the window. She also called Omari, who lived next door. "Omari, look outside your window. Tell me what you see."

Omari placed the phone on the table and looked outside his window.

Jill heard the scream and the words "Oh sweat."

Afrolena ran to the window and pulled back the curtains. Afrolena saw Omari run out the building with his cell phone in hand, talking to someone. Leon was gone. She looked outside and saw Leon running down the normally quiet Newark block.

"Oh my god," yelled Leon.

The grisly details of the crime were in plain sight of Omari and Leon. A lifeless male, who appeared to be in his thirties lay face down on a bed of blood soaked leaves that covered the mica speckled sidewalk.

Officers arrived at the scene of the crime shortly after Omari placed a call to them. The precinct was located minutes away from the house. The officers turned him over to find that his face was disfigured and covered with blood. The blood had not yet dried up on his face. One could safely assume that the crime recently occurred. It was obvious that he was stabbed multiple times.

From the way the body fell onto the cement, it appeared as though the man attempted to flee from the car. His leg was twisted. His buttons were off his shirt, a sign that some type of struggle occurred. A nine-inch butcher knife covered in blood was in plain view on the front passenger seat of the car. The blood soaked knife was covered with a washcloth. A lone glove and a decorative statue were found on the front seat of the car.

The paramedics arrived. Their attempts to revive the victim were useless. The male victim had no pulse. The paramedics verified that there was no life left in the victim. The urgency of rushing the victim to the hospital was quickly diminished. The customary white cloth was pulled over his head. The six-foot-tall black male victim was placed on a gurney and wheeled into the ambulance. The police officer retrieved the knife and a bloody statue from the car. The officers advised Omari to get into the patrol car.

"Uhh!" Omari's startled look silently spoke his feelings.

Omari said, "I have no qualms with going to the police station, but we did not see anything. Leon can stay behind."

"One of the officers responded, I know you. You own an art business, don't you? This is strange. We need to question you."

"I don't know much, Officer. My friend Jill called me because she noticed something strange going on outside. I looked out the window and saw the body of the man. The lifeless body was quickly carted off in the ambulance. It was obvious that he needed immediate attention. Prior to reaching the body, I placed a 911 call to the police. When I touched the body it was cold. The blood on his body was still fresh. I felt no pulse."

"Is this the weapon you observed?"

The knife, covered in blood, was held up in the air so that Omari and Leon could see the knife.

"Yes, Officer, that appears to be the weapon I observed laying near the body."

"Did you notice this statue?"

Omari gasped! "Ahhh!" A long wave of silence filled the air. "No, I did not…but I am familiar with that statue. The statue is from the boutique. Officer, you are holding a million dollars in your hand."

"We need your telephone number for our records. You might be called on later to testify.

You are a material witness."

"Witness?" said Omari in a slightly elevated and highly questioning tone.

"I did not see the crime."

"But you saw the body. That alone is enough for us to question you."

"Now there is this added twist. You are telling me that this statue is usually on display in your boutique."

"Yes, Officer, give that to me. He must have stolen it."

"Omari, if we determine that this statue belongs to you, you will get it back."

Omari took note of the badge number and name of the police officer.

Omari silently prayed. "*Lord Jesus please hear my silent pray. Let the police return this item to me.*"

"I need to call my lawyer immediately. The presence of my statue casts a whole different picture on this crime. Just how long do you intend to hold onto my statue?"

"I know you're not holding onto my statue for life."

Leon ran to Omari and whispered, "Just be cool. I understand your unvoiced concerns."

Officer Hammond responded, "Are you trying to insinuate something?"

Omari humbled himself. "No sir."

"So you want to question Omari, but you have not demonstrated that he and I are material witnesses, Officer," said Leon. "I am a lawyer."

"You are a lawyer. Well, I hope you are a criminal lawyer cause your friend, Omari, needs a criminal lawyer," said Officer Hammond.

"This statue is allegedly owned by Omari Boutique. That puts a whole different spin on this crime."

"I need you to get into the back seat of the squad car, Omari."

The plastic bag contained the knife, a phone book, a pair of eyeglasses, a cell phone, and some cut-up coke straws with some white residue in the straw. The statue was placed in a separate storage container.

"This is interesting. Seems like a simple crime to resolve, but many times something simple turns into a lengthy investigation."

Omari obeyed the officer's order and quietly slid into the back seat of the squad car.

Omari said, "You're Officer Hammond's partner? I know you." Omari glanced at the officer's name badge. Officer Tomlinson?"

A puzzled look could be seen on Tomlinson's face. "Omari, Omari…where have I heard that name? I know that name. Aren't you the owner of Omari Boutique?"

"Yes, I am the proud owner of Omari Boutique."

"That is my statue. I have receipts and can prove it."

Tomlinson said, "Right now we need you to cooperate. You are lucky I recognized you. I'm not going to cuff you, but the presence of this statue is highly questionable. You are lucky that I am not one of those hot headed officers. You did not know that the statue was stolen from the boutique until now?"

"Actually Officer, I knew it was missing. I reported it to the police and my insurance company. You might want to check your files. I will provide the police department with proof that I am the owner of the bloody statue."

An Arduous Task?

"All right, Carolyn what do we have here?" said Dr. Ucorn.

"This male victim was stabbed. We found the murder weapon at the scene of the crime."

Carolyn, an expert in the field of forensic science, began the arduous task of examining the body and crime scene evidence.

Dr. Ucorn folded the white sheet to the waist of the crime victim. The blood-soaked torso was revealed. Dr. Ucorn officially pronounced the victim DOA then performed an autopsy. While inspecting the body, Dr. Ucorn recorded his findings on his cell phone.

"Let's see, what do we have here, Dr. Ucorn?"

"Carolyn, a preliminary review of the body indicates that victim number 1251 died as a result of being stabbed multiple times. There are a total of ten puncture wounds to the victim's face and body. A wound on his right hand could possibly indicate that he attempted to shield the knife from penetrating his body. The blow that ultimately killed the man was a direct hit to the jugular vein from a knife. Judging from the position of the wounds, it appears that the assailant was left-handed."

Carolyn performed a microscopic analysis of the fibers that were dusted from the car. She also conducted a test on a lone strand of hair that was found on the victim. The coroner sent the silky blonde hair fiber to the lab for DNA testing. These vital tests could possibly lead to a break in the case. Victim number 1251 had coarse black hair. The victim was black.

Since no one saw the assailants, one could not safely assume that the hair belonged to the assailant. It could be the hair of an unidentified person who may have had close contact with the victim. Dr. Ucorn removed the solo blonde hair strand up with a tweezers and noticed that the roots were gray.

"Who knows?" said Dr. Ucorn. "Could be that the dead man experienced a night of ecstasy with a hooker." I speculate that this romp in the hay and night of ecstasy lead to a violent fight. During the altercation he was killed."

His assistant laughed. Dr. Ucorn often made up wild stories about how murder victims might have been killed. Ucorn's wild imagination conjured up tales of how victims of crime died. After a while, he kept a scoreboard of the victims who passed through his arms. He compared the actual crime story to his wild suppositions of what actually led to the death of his patients. Right now, he is averaging a 65 percent accuracy rate.

Carolyn suggested that the presence of an expensive art piece indicates that this was a struggle over a stolen piece of art. "Dr. Ucorn, there is evidence of a blunt blow to the side of the victims' head. This art piece has to be returned to the evidence room immediately."

Dr. Ucorn collected a blood sample from the victim and ordered a series of tests, including drug toxicology tests. Chief Summerlyn phoned the forensic lab. Summerlyn spoke directly to Dr. Ucorn, with whom he had established a professional working relationship.

"Ucorn this is Chief Summerlyn. How close are you to completing the results of the toxicology and other reports on victim number 1251? I need you to put a rush on the tests. When you complete the test, please send the results to the precinct via private courier."

Dr. Ucorn assured Summerlyn that the results should be received in the precinct within twenty-four hours. Ucorn informed Summerlyn that he completed the examination and was in the process of writing the report.

An unexpected twist turned up during the examination. The victim was wounded in the left temporal lobe at close range. The wound fit perfectly with the shape of the statue. Had he lived, he would have suffered damage to his speech. Also, he would have been unable to recognize familiar faces.

The wound was fresh. It appeared to be approximately ten to twelve hours old.

"This confirms that the killing occurred sometime during the night," said Ucorn.

"Mmm," said Summerlyn, "perhaps there was more than one assailant."

Make sure you complete the drug and alcohol toxicology as we found cut up plastic straws with cocaine residue inside the pants pockets of the victim."

"The blood alcohol concentration test is complete. The victim had a high alcohol concentration his bloodstream. The victim had a .39 level of alcohol content in his blood stream. This level of alcohol content in the blood stream can lead to unconsciousness, severe central nervous system dysfunction, impaired breathing, and loss of bladder control. We also discovered evidence of cocaine in his system."

Ucorn summoned the police chief. The autopsy revealed that the victim was also shot in the head with a .22 caliber gun. Officer Lynne advised the dispatcher to inform the homicide unit to search for a .22 caliber bullet.

"I need you to return to the marked crime scene as it appeared that there may be a gun in the immediate vicinity of the crime."

"Once you come within five blocks of the crime scene, I suggest that you drive with your silent alarm on."

Four police cars were dispatched to Grafton Avenue. The block was quiet. There was only one person in sight. The police observed a man dressed in baggy knee-length blue denim shorts walking leisurely down the street. A total of eight officers proceeded to comb the area. The area was taped off with yellow tape that read "Do Not Cross—Crime Scene Investigation."

Neighbors were aroused from their sleep when they heard the blaring sounds of police sirens. Hearing unknown voices in the darkness of night prompted many people to look out their windows. Some were bold enough to raise their shades. Slowly, heads began to appear in the windows. Some residents gingerly moved their curtains aside so that they could peep through the side of their windows without being seen.

One lady, who remained in hiding, screamed, "Hey, Officer, I saw a lone man run in that direction—over there, where you found the body." She shielded her face from view and pointed. "Check the bushes to the right, it seems like he tossed an object in that direction."

The officers eventually located a small .22 caliber pistol in the area that pointed to.

The officer lifted the gun with a pen and gently placed it in a plastic evidence bag. The gun was found in the middle of a bush. It was apparent that the gun man tossed the gun with such forced that it was lodged partially into the soil. The policemen phoned the report into police headquarters.

"Okay. Officers you have clearance to return home, but prior to leaving, please post the reward poster up. You indicated a lady who appeared to live in the neighborhood might know more about the crime. Let's see if the reward money will flush her out."

"Great job," said Chief Summerlyn. Within twenty-four hours of notifying the community of the manhunt and posting the reward notice for information that might lead to an arrest, five witnesses presented valuable information to the police. Chief Summerlyn, a highly decorated officer with a multitude of awards, was known to be fair and friendly. He was an expert in police investigations and training. His unit received many awards for solving a number of high-profile investigations. Chief Summerlyn was hired to address the recent increase in violent crimes. His previous employment as the deputy chief of police in Chicago, a city that has a high rate of violent crimes, provided him with the skills he needed to employ in the Newark City police department. Officers assigned to this elite unit were highly skilled and seasoned.

To be a member of the elite Summerlyn squad is an honor and a privilege. If one wanted to apply for a job in Secret Services, they were nearly guaranteed a position once it was known that Chief Summerlyn trained them.

The gun was immediately whisked into the forensic lab. There was a round of live ammunition in the gun, and only two bullets were left in the chamber. Henry, a ballistics specialist, performed the necessary test. The results showed that these bullets were fired from the gun that was retrieved from the scene of the crime. This advanced method of examination was not used by many police departments. This method of testing was expensive but yielded highly accurate results. The results returned in a matter of minutes.

Chief Summerlyn was instrumental in developing the test. Summerlyn attended the University of California and received a bachelor's degree in chemistry. Upon graduating from his class, he decided to take the police officer test. His family was known in law enforcement. His uncle was appointed to the United States Drug Enforcement Task Bureau. He held one of the highest-ranking law enforcement positions in the United States.

Summerlyn advised the medical examiner that shells were never located at the scene. The examiner informed Summerlyn that there was a need to locate the shells. Detective Newman was instructed to return to the scene.

It was nearly 8:00 p.m. when Detective Newman arrived at the crime scene with a metal detector and a flashlight. Newman carefully combed through the area, leaving no spot uncovered. Finally, just as he reached the end of the property line, he was able to locate a metal object that was lodged into the soil. He used tweezers to dislodge the bullet from the ground. He carefully sealed and placed the shell into a secure plastic bag.

Newman informed his commanding officer that he located the shell. "There is a possibility that there is another shell," said Chief Summerlyn."

"Did you examine the area with a fine-tooth comb?"

"Yes, sir, I did. I only found one bullet casing."

Officer Summerlyn responded, "Then come back to the station immediately Detective Newman."

Officer Newman responded, "Over and out."

Newman drove the black unmarked Ford SUV into the station lot. Newman's partner for the night, Caesar, rode in the back. Newman cruised down the street in his unmarked police car. He noticed a crowd of girls dressed in provocative clothing fit for a prostitute. They paraded down the street in high heels, bare skin, and skimpy miniskirts.

Newman's thoughts headed to the ozone layer. Nowadays, "hooker wear" is the going thing. Cheeks hanging out everywhere. It's not so easy to decipher the hookers from ladies just walking down the avenue anymore. That one is looking real hot.

Newman stopped at the traffic light. He heard a female voice calling out from the street.

"Hey, mister, are you looking for a hot date?"

Newman responded, "Yeah right. How much does that date cost?"

"For you, dear, it is free," shouted the lady of the night.

Newman sped away when the light turned green.

"What's up with that?" said Deanna.

"You're selling yourself cheap. You're not catching no bait tonight." Linda was the new kid on the strip. She was fresh meat.

Linda said, "Deanna he smelled like a cop to me. So I dropped the line. This is my first night out, and I'm not ready to go to jail tonight."

"But that is five missed call, Linda. Your pimp will get mad at you if you don't bring the cash in. Step to the side, Linda, I'll show you how to do it."

Deanna wore a low-cut shirt that exposed her size-D cups. She strutted across the street and leaned into a car that was parked on the side of the road.

"Hey, babe, you sure are looking real juicy. They call me Juicy Fruit, and I can make a grown man shriver."

The man blushed and instructed Deanna to get in the car. Within five minutes both of them departed from the car and walked hand in hand to the fleabag hotel.

Linda was amazed. She sucked her teeth and muttered to one of the ladies, "I heard Deanna is the queen of this strip." The jealous lady of the night sucked her teeth and continued to chew briskly on a stale piece of wintergreen gum.

Newman and Newman's very snoopy German Sheppard police dog, Caesar, finally arrived at the newly built police station. Caesar barked once to alert the department of their arrival. Caesar followed Newman into the station.

"Congratulation, the work that you did on this case is superb."

The bullets and gun were dusted for prints and resulted in a negative finding for prints. The impounded car was thoroughly searched. Caesar was brought to the scene of the crime to sniff for drugs. Caesar sniffed out a small bag of what appears to be cocaine.

Newman muttered under his breath, "I hate these type of cases, makes one scratch their head looking for a motive." Just as he finished drinking his coffee and was about to leave the room, the forensic expert came into the lunchroom.

"We were finally able to identify the body of John Doe as being Joe Marvin Pention."

"Joe Pention—otherwise known in the street as King Pention," said Detective Newman.

"You know him? The mucker. He always found legal ways to hoard money."

"Yes," said Newman, "he was a well-known street hustler in the South Bronx. He had a stable of girls and sold drugs sells. At least we have a few possible motives for the crimes."

Newman departed from the room and signed out for the evening. In an effort to unravel the crime Newman stayed three hours beyond his appointed shift. Caesar sat quietly by his desk.

Newman steadily worked on that case for months. The trails led no place; it was a cold case. No suspect was arrested. Newman consulted with his superior.

"I think we have worked on this case long enough. Unfortunately, some crimes are never resolved. Chief, this case fits into that category."

Chief Summerlyn concurred it was time to close the case.

"Put the red unresolved crime stamp on the outside of the record, Newman."

Detective Joseph Newman Sr. pulled into the driveway of his private house, located in an exclusive neighborhood in Maplewood, NJ. His five-bedroom, four-bath Tudor brick home was custom designed and built by a well-known builder. His wife, Alice, was in the kitchen cooking when he entered the home. Detective Newman quietly closed the door and tip toed to her. He planted a big kiss on her neck.

"Alice jumped. Oh god! You scared me. My dear, I told you about that tip toe act."

Joseph chuckled, "The food smells good."

"Baked chicken, rice, and carrots cooked just the way you like it," said Alice.

Their three kids ran down stairs to greet their father. Newman greeted each one of them.

"Dad, see what I drew in my art class," said Mary. Mary proudly held the painting in the air. "I made it just for you, Dad."

"That's beautiful, Mary." "How about we take this painting to Omari Boutique and have it framed. We'll go to Omari Boutique on Saturday. I think that painting will look nice in the entry hallway.

"Harold and Joseph, how was gym class today?"

"Today, we practiced on the uneven parallel bars. Tomorrow we will begin classes on the pommel horse," said Joseph.

Harold and Joseph's aspirations to compete on the Olympics gymnastic team inched closer to becoming a reality when they won the New Jersey state championship gold medal for overall gymnasts.

Joseph was the outspoken child. He was also a highly talented saxophonist. He composed and arranged a musical tune entitled, "*The Sun Sets in the East*" when he was twelve years old. The song was entered in a contest. Joseph was thrilled when he found out that he won the contest. Joseph was a child prodigy.

Four-year-old Mary was a bundle of energy. Harold generally went with the flow of things. You never heard any lip from him. Joseph was unpredictable.

As promised, Newman took Mary to Omari Boutique on Saturday. "Dad, how long will it take for the picture frame to be completed?"

"I don't know."

Once they were inside, Mary immediately pointed to a frame on the side.

Jill asked Mary if she was sure that that was the frame she wanted. "Here's another frame that might look nice too."

Mary was still stuck on the plain wooden frame that she picked out. "How long will it take to be finished?" she asked Mary.

"I can have this ready for you in three hours."

Mary smiled from ear to ear. Jill praised her artwork and advised her father that this piece should be submitted in a children's contest that she knew about.

"That would be nice. Where can we get the information for the contest?"

Jill handed Newman a card that contained the website address.

"Daddy, please, can we enter my art into the contest?"

"I don't see a problem with entering your artwork in the contest, but of course we have to discuss it with your mother."

"Come on Dad, just say yes Dad—please."

"Okay, Mary you can put the art in the contest."

Joseph Newman, Sr. and Mary shopped in the various neighborhood stores. Three hours went by fast. Newman decided to drive Mary home as she was tired. He returned to Omari Boutique without Mary.

Immediately upon entering the galley, Newman noticed Det. Swoop. "Hey, Det. Swoop, what's up, you got the scoop? Long time no see."

"I see you are still a comedian, Newman." They gave each other a hug and a fist bump.

Det. Swoop and Newman worked together in the fifth precinct five years ago. They were rookies. They graduated from the same police academy. Realizing that Det. Swoop was in the midst of a deep conversation with Omari, Joseph kept the conversation brief. Newman called out to Jill.

"Hey, Jill, is the picture frame ready? My daughter is excited. She takes after her mother. Her mother studied fine art in college."

"Yes it is. Hold on, let me get it." Jill went to the back storage room and returned with the framed painting.

"This is lovely, Jill. You did the framing?"

"No, Sean did it." said Jill.

"Sean hides in the back. Few people know he is even here."

"I'm glad you are happy with the framing, Newman. We believe in treating our customers as though they are family. A happy customer is a returning customer. That's why our motto is *It's in the Bag*. We guarantee that we will sell your art, book and buried treasure. In fact, we are going to put *It in the Bag*. Of course certain conditions do apply. It is important that we maintain high morals, fast and efficient service to our customers."

Before wrapping the frame up Jill requested that they examine the framing and sign the release for the artwork, a piece that was completed on matted canvas board with oil paint.

Detective Newman shouted to Swoop as he departed from the store, "Man, I sure would love to work with you again."

Detective Swoop responded, "I see you like art."

"Yes, Swoop, I love art so much that I decided to become certified in art theft investigator. I recently completed Smithsonian Institutes postgraduate certificate program in art crime."

"Mmm—that's interesting. I completed my art theft certificate at the Smithsonian too. Seems like we are walking on the same path. I was recruited by the FBI Art Crime Team to work with the elite FBI team. I turned it down."

"I can't tell you what I am working on but I'm sure you would enjoy working with me on this case. I'm going to ask Chief Summerlyn if you can be assigned to the case—I need help. Just wait a minute."

Swoop immediately phoned Chief Summerlyn. Within seconds he received permission to work with Newman on the Omari art theft case.

Det. Newman said, "Swoop you are now my partner on the Omari art theft case. You will receive a text from Chief Summerlyn to advise you of your new assignment."

Newman immediately received the text message.

Omari continued his conversation with Det. Ted Swoop. Swoop asked Det. Newman to join the conservation. Omari went on to state that he recently noticed that a number of paintings he purchased were incorrectly numbered. The numbers did not correspond with the numbers on the invoice.

Omari showed Det. Swoop and Newman one of the paintings that he purchased. Det. Swoop spoke in detail about the not so complex number system on artwork. The lower the number of reprints of an art piece, the higher the value. This Dean Mitchell artwork has a duplicate number. Dean Mitchell, a painter who is well-known for his figurative works, landscapes, and still life are painted in watercolor. He has won numerous awards. The boutique specializes in the sale of art that represents the thoughts, feelings, culture and heritage of people of color.

"Omari, I would like to take this painting with me. I'm going to show this painting to the chief of police."

"Okay, but you will have to sign a release for the painting, Swoop."

Detective Swoop said, "I'll sign the release but this type of crime is tolerated. Art theft is seldom resolved."

"Art theft is usually done either to resell the piece for profit, ransom or to secure loans. This form of theft is known as art-napping. In order to secure your beautiful art displays

I suggest that you hire a guard because your collection is extensive. I also noticed that your paintings are not hung on wires. You can best secure your collection by hanging paintings with thick wire and locks. Your electronic alarm system seems on par with industry. You might want to consider sending your staff to the Smithsonian Institution's National Conference on Cultural Property Protection in D.C. The Association for Research into Crimes against Art or ARCA offers a postgraduate certificate program in art crime and cultural heritage protection in Italy."

"Why is art theft tolerated?" asked Omari.

Det. Swoop responded, "Well, Robert K. Witman, an expert in the field of art theft and former head of the FBI Art Crime Team until his retirement in 2008, knew that art is a victimless crime."

"However, Omari, in this case there was intent to harm. That's why we are thoroughly investigating this matter."

Newman was given a number of task to complete by Det. Swoop. Newman was given two weeks to complete the task. The first item on the list was to find out the actual number of paintings sold. The second item on the list was to find out where the painting was ordered from, the shipment date and the name of the manufacturer who distributed the painting is needed."

Newman departed from the store. It would be the first of many art theft crimes he would investigate.

Newman turned into his driveway.

"Mommy, mommy Daddy is home!"

Mary and her mother ran to the driveway. "Let me see, shouted Mary." Mary quickly tore off the brown paper from the piece. Her mother gasped. "It's beautiful," said Alice.

Joseph Newman informed his wife that Jill really likes this painting. "She told me about an art contest for children. I want to enter this painting in the contest."

Mary jumped up and down. She ran into the house singing a made up tune, "I'm going to be entered into a contest. I'm going to be entered into a contest."

Newman overheard her and cracked up. He said, "How fast can we submit her, and how will we ship her." Her mom cracked up too.

The Revolving Door

Det. Swoop carried the painting into the police station as promised. Swoop informed Chief Summerlyn that he will have additional information for him in two weeks.

Thanks for assigning Newman to the case. He's my partner—I know his work."

"I know his work too Det. Swoop.

The next day Det. Swoop phoned Omari. "Hi, Omari I need to return to the gallery. Please provide a list of all customers, their addresses and phone numbers. I expect to arrive at the boutique around noon.

As planned Swoop arrived at the boutique on time. He examined the paintings that were on display in the gallery and received the customer list, as well as all orders that were placed within the last years. At first, there appeared to be nothing unusual—until they noticed that there were two similar names on the roster. Swoop advised Omari that his cooperation in the case was extremely helpful.

Wednesday was truly gifted. She increased sales in the store and was credited with the development of their customer loyalty program.

She arrived at the store just as Ted Swoop was exiting. Det. Swoop nearly stopped in his tracks when he saw Wednesday. Wednesday and Det. Swoop's eyes met. The chemistry between the two of them could not be denied.

Det. Swoop slowly walked towards Wednesday. He said, "What's your name?"

"My name is Wednesday and you are?"

"My name is Detective Ted Swoop."

Det. Swoop, was dressed in a well-decorated uniform. He was six feet tall and built like a football player. He towered over Wednesday. Swoop proudly wore his multiple awards for bravery on his chest. He was well-known throughout the country as he was directly responsible for the arrest and apprehension of a number of America's top wanted fugitives.

He became the go to man. Because of his charismatic persona, he was offered a spot as a commentator on a cable television station that featured high-profile crimes. The show became a smash hit. Det. Swoop's guest speakers included well-known experts in the field who discussed hot topics on his show. The case of Neil Posterling catapulted Det. Swoop to stardom. Posterling, a well-known fugitive, name has been on the top of the most wanted list for the past five years. Some thought he would never be apprehended. He was wanted for armed robbery, grand theft auto, extortion, and money laundering.

His rap sheet was as tall as the Empire State building. At the age of twenty-seven, Posterling's rap record surpassed the records of the most senior criminals. Neil was a master of disguise and an expert in pulling off highly complex crimes. His demise came when he resorted to criminalizing his family.

In order to escape authorities, he often dressed up like a woman. He traveled from state to state and slithered through the state lines with the ease of a snake. His final chapter ended in a hail of bullets as he tried to escape the NYC Police in a stolen vehicle. Headlines of his death appeared on local and national television stations. Being that this art case was tied to a possible international art ring, Det. Swoop and Det. Newman were assigned to the case.

Wednesday slowly strolled through the store in her high heels and hot, but professional, miniskirt, pretending not to stare. "May I help you, officer?" asked Wednesday.

Det. Swoop was lost for words. Omari quietly observed the encounter and sensed that this brief meeting would lead to a relationship that would last for a lifetime.

"I already took care of business. I just wanted to say hello to you," said Det. Swoop. He threw Wednesday a quick, sexy look and proceeded out the door.

"Omari, who is that guy?"

"He is investigating a situation here. I could see the chemistry between you two. Det. Swoop was recently featured on a nightly news show because of his involvement in apprehending one of America's most wanted criminals."

"Mmm," responded Wednesday. "He looks yummy to me."

"Yummy. Now that is an interesting way to say you are intrigued by him. There appears to be some pirating of paintings going on."

Afrolena stood in the background holding a stack of papers. With a sigh, Afrolena proclaimed. "There is never a dull moment here."

Suddenly the phone rang. Omari picked up the phone. He immediately recognized Det. Swoop's voice.

"Hello, Swoop, is there something you forgot?"

"Yep, I want to talk to Wednesday."

Wordlessly, Omari passed the phone to Wednesday.

"Hi, Wednesday, I want to know if you are doing anything around five o'clock tonight. I would like to invite you to dinner."

Wednesday's impish smile seemed to radiate across the room.

"Tell you what, Det. Swoop, I'll pass for tonight as I have an important meeting to attend, but are you free to spend time with me on another day?"

"Wednesday you are stunning. I am lost for words. Omari has nothing but good things to say about you. I really want to get to know you. Ahh— I know this must sound crazy but I don't know how to tell you this—is there really something called love at first sight. Because if there is well—seems I got hit with it today."

"Yes," said Wednesday, "next Friday will work for me."

"How about we go on the Smooth Jazz Cruise? Will Downing is playing next Friday."

"Sounds fine to me. I prefer to go on the sunset cruise, Ted."

"Sure, Wednesday. I figured since Omari Boutique features jazz, I could not go wrong asking you to hold my hand while Will Downing sings. I'll pick you up at the boutique around 4:00 p.m. That way we will get a good parking spot and seat on the boat."

"I have to ask for early dismissal from work." "Omari," shouted Wednesday as she hung up the phone. "May I leave work at four on Friday?"

"What's up, Wednesday, you got a hot date?" Omari laughed. Unknown to Wednesday, he was instrumental in setting up that date.

"Yes it's Ted Swoop, every woman's dream."

Omari pretended to fan himself. He chuckled as he pronounced, "Oh, you got the hot one—

You go, girl."

"Okay, Wednesday, enjoy your date with Ted."

Wednesday phoned Ted. "Hi Ted, Omari said it's okay to leave early on Friday." Wednesday's excitement could not be contained.

"Great," responded Ted. "I can't wait to see you."

Wednesday hung up the phone and returned to the show room floor. Wednesday asked Jill if she could begin work at two o'clock at the boutique on Friday.

Jill agreed to work for her.

"Where are you going, Wednesday?" asked Omari.

"Umm…to see Will Downing with Ted."

"Don't forget to get Will Downing's business card. We would love to have him perform at Omari Boutique."

"What do you think I should wear, Omari?"

Omari said, "You look great in anything. If you want to capture his attention, I suggest that you wear red. Red against you skin tone works perfectly. Tell you what, take the whole day off. I'll pay you."

Wednesday kissed Omari on the cheek.

Susan jokingly said, "Watch it sister. That's my man."

As promised, Jill arrived at the store at two o'clock to relieve Wednesday. It was a slow day. Five o'clock came too slowly for Jill. Jill kept looking at her watch. She set the store alarm before leaving the store. She than escaped into the warm air of summer. Her new red, two-seater sports convertible often grabbed the eyes of many. Jill flipped down the automatic convertible top, lit a cigarette, and turned on the radio to her favorite jazz station. Her favorite songstress, Phyllis Hyman, played on the radio.

"I was just a rider in the storm—I needed love to keep me standing strong. I was going insane until I found you, boy…" Hyman could do no wrong. Jill's voice filled the car. "The answer, boy, is you." Jill sang at the top of her lungs. "When you touch me, there's something deep inside."

Jill often considered taking voice lessons, but being a wife and mother occupied much of her time.

Her children ran to the car and greeted her. Rose's childhood innocence and excitement could not be contained. "Mommy, Mommy, what did you bring home for me today?"

Jill spoiled her children. Jill jumped out the car and kissed both of them. Rose giggled.

"Your kiss is good enough for me."

"Oh, Mommy," said Eric, "Did you forget that tomorrow is the African-American Heritage festival? We always see all our friends there."

"No, Little Sean, I did not forget—Little Sean, we will go to the festival tomorrow."

Little Sean was the nickname Jill chose for her son. Jill nicknamed Eric, Little Sean. Jill loved Sean Connery's 007 character in James Bond movies. She secretly hoped that her son would be the next generation's James Bond. With that in mind, she decided to name her unborn son, Sean. Leon strongly objected. In fact, Leon and Jill had a huge fight in the maternity ward over his name. Leon ultimately convinced Jill that their son should be named Eric because his great-grandfather's name was Eric. Jill finally agreed to name their son Eric but insisted that his middle name be

Sean. The name stuck. Much to Leon's chagrin, everybody calls Eric, Little Sean.

Jill retrieved the mail from the mailbox and noticed that there was a letter from "*The Revolving Door Show*," a television game show that everyone enjoyed. As soon as she got inside, she gingerly opened the letter and screamed, "I won."

Jill's mother came out of her room. Jill jumped up from the couch and handed her mother the letter.

"Dear Jill,

We are pleased to advise you that based on your response to our essay question on why you should be a contestant on *The Revolving Door Show*, we have enclosed five tickets for you and your family. The show will be filmed in NYC on August 1 at 7:00 p.m. It is a live taping. We request that you dress in bright colors because we feel bright colors film better. We look forward to meeting you and request that you confirm your attendance by June 30. Jill, you are welcome to bring up to five guests to the live taping. We look forward to meeting you and your family, but if for some reason your guests cannot attend, please contact us.

Sincerely,
Mark Lewis, Executive Producer
"*The Revolving Door Show*"

"We don't need a house now," said Grandma Louise, who was often called Grandma L. "That's all right. Maybe we can donate the house to our favorite cause or to a working-class family who has a vision and a dream," said Jill.

"Well, Jill, I hope you win. This moment of fame just might lead to a new beginning for a family in need of a new house."

Jill and her family accepted the offer. This smash hit show was built on the foundation of entering a revolving door, snatching a question off the door, and answering the first question correctly. The stage was set up with four revolving doors for four contestants. Each contestant has to open the window, flip it down, and uncover the hidden message. There is a small window of time during which they must unscramble words or correctly answer a question. If the answer is correct, the contestant advances to the third and final stage. At this stage, the contestant enters the attic. Blindfolds were placed on the remaining contestants just prior to their arrival into the attic, where a large treasure chest that contained five coins with different prizes was located. If the contestant retrieves the gold coin, he or she wins the grand prize— a house of their choosing within the price limits. Winners were given three months to locate a house of their dreams.

The show contracted with a number of large real estate companies. Excerpts of the contestants shopping trips and final decision were filmed and presented during the show.

Perhaps the funniest clip showed an agent accidentally knocking down the butler's door in a vacant house.

The day finally came for Jill to attempt to conquer The Revolving Door. She shook her husband up from sleep.

"Come on, Leon, it's time to wake up. We don't want to miss the plane. Mom is already up. Eric and Rose wake up. Today we are the stars."

Excitement filled the air. The long black limousine with custom vanity plates arrived at their door and transported them to Kennedy Airport. Eric and Rose never flew in an airplane. Nor had they ever visited California. They were full of energy. Jill purchased a trivia book many months before the show so that she could refresh her memory on important facts in the United States and abroad.

The announcer, in a robust voice, shouted with much animated energy, "Welcome to The Revolving Door show." He introduced the contestants and briefly explained the rules of the game. Jill wore a casual pair of pants, flat shoes, and a brightly colored shirt. Each contestant eagerly awaited the sound of the bell.

Contestant number 1, a young male, who appeared to be in his early twenties, quickly darted into the right door, he quickly detached the question and ran out of the door, handing the sealed envelope to the assistant. Contestant number 2, a middle-aged female, could not quite get the beat or timing of the revolutions of the door. The buzzer rang before she got up the nerve to try to enter the revolving door. She waved her hand at the door and walked away from the stage in disgust. Contestant number three looked like a body builder. The door revolved, he flew into the right entry way and detached the envelope. Jill studied the first two revolutions of the door and flew in just before the buzzer rang. She retrieved the question.

"All right, three of you have made it through the Revolving Door."

The audience prompted by the producer shouted revolving door!"

All contestants stood at the podium. The podium contained a big red button.

"Contestants, are you ready? Who was the first man to land on the moon?"

They were given three answers to pick from. "Congratulations! All of you answered the question correctly." The stagehands flashed a card that contained the right answer so that the audience is unison could scream "Neil Armstrong."

"All right, are you ready for the next level?" The audience shouted, "Yes."

"It's time to—" the audience joined in— "flip the window."

Bob Larken, the host of the show announced, "These remaining contestants must now step up to the line, open the flip-down window, and unscramble the hidden words. Are you ready?" The audience cheered, "Yes."

"You have one minute to flip and answer. You may begin when the buzzer sounds. Write the word on the electronic pad and display it when the second buzzer rings."Contestant number one and three correctly answered the question.

"The rest of you have advanced to the final round. Are you ready? These lovely ladies will blindfold you and escort you to the attic, where there is a large treasure chest that contains coins. Each coin reveals a different prize. If you pull out the gold coin, you win the Grand Prize, a house of your choosing within price limits. That's right, we are not giving out mansions; that's the other show."

The audience bust into a round of laughter.

The music played.

"Ladies, please take off the contestants' blindfolds. Contestant number 1, you won an all expense trip to Hawaii." He was elated.

Jill held the gold coin up in the air and shouted, "Oh my god!" Her family ran to the stage, and the announcer shouted, "Congratulations!"

The audience cheered and shouted, "You won a house." Jill cried. "We have decided to donate the house to our favorite charity, Habitat for Humanity."

A male voice from the audience shouted, "Wait a minute." Leon stepped to the stage.

"I'm the man of the house, you won and we are keeping the house."

The audience cheered. The lights on the stage were slowly faded to black and the final show jingle played.

Leon and Afrolena explored the rest of the sights in the area and then flew to San Francisco. They loved the Mediterranean style homes.

They traveled in a rental car into Sausalito, an area that is known for its art galleries and dining. Jill and Leon purchased an original painting by a local artist. The red-colored mountains stood out as did the evergreens mixed with cacti. The children were mesmerized. Eric said, "I can't believe cacti can live together with evergreens."

Eric and Rose could not believe the size of the trees in the redwood forest. The Pacific coast was untouchable. Its natural shoreline and waves instill peacefulness in your soul. Their trip was relaxing; one that they would remember for years. They all but forgotten the strange and mysterious phone calls. Their trip ended when they boarded the red-eye back to New York. As they waited for their luggage at the baggage claim area, a tall gentleman approached them from behind. Leon turned around when he felt hot air and the sound of breathing on his neck. He quickly realized that the gentleman breathing down his neck was one of his partners from the law firm.

"I heard you were arriving so I thought you just might need a ride home. How did it go?" asked Mr. Berger.

"Everything was fine. In fact, Jill won.

"Come on, Eric and Rose, wake up we are home."

The ride home from the airport was uneventful. Until Leon realized the painting they purchased was left in the airport.

"Oh, I don't remember seeing the boxed up painting that we purchased from the art gallery, Susan."

"You are right. We were the first to arrive at the baggage claim and the last to leave. I did not see the box, Leon. We'll have to report it to airport security and phone the airline."

"Leon called airport security."

"Port of Newark Liberty Airport Security, Liz speaking."

"Hello, Liz my name is Leon Sullivan. My and wife and arrived on the flight that from California—Southwest Airlines flight number 629, a box that we checked in never arrived at baggage claim."

"Let me check into that for you."

Leon heard the sound of the typing. After a few minutes Liz returned to the phone. "The good news is we located your box. As a courtesy to you we can send the package directly to you. We are sorry for any inconvenience. Please accept our apologies and we will send you a twenty percent discount coupon that can be used on any Southwest flight. This coupon is good for a year.

Leon thanked Liz and promptly hung up the phone.

The taxi finally arrived at their home.

Jill checked the answering machine. There were tons of hang ups. But the tenth message contained a mysterious voice. "Jill, I remember you from the museum—" Then silence and a click.

Leon immediately saved the surreptitious message so that the police could hear it. He didn't want to worry his wife, so he debated on whether or not to tell her. She was in the shower when he received the mysterious message. Leon was known for his ability to stand in the eye of a storm and remain undaunted. Leon's calmness was recognized by many. People respected his advice and ability to make rational decisions, even when the world seemed to be falling apart in front of his eyes.

Deciding that his wife should know, Leon replayed the message for Jill to hear. Jill was shocked. They called the police. They were instructed to proceed to the police station.

They were promptly escorted into a private room. Officer Newman asked Jill if she remembered any weird occurrences or any strange people following them. Jill immediately thought about the strange occurrences at the museum.

"The best I can remember is that it was a nice summer day."

"Did you attend any special events that might help us to pinpoint the day?"

Jill hesitated at first. She than realized that she and the kids attended a special program at the children's interactive museum—the *Mr. Giggles* show.

"Great, we can go back to the museum and ask when they featured the show."

Jill described the man as being white and approximately five feet eleven inches tall, with a bland head, and he appeared to weigh over two hundred pounds. He wore a light purple shirt and tightly fitted jeans. Detective Newman asked if there were any distinguishing marks on his body.

"None that I can remember. All I know is he stalked us. I even heard a male voice call out my name. I dodged into a darkened alcove with the kids because I realized he was following us. Once we hid, he walked past us and then I walked behind him so I could keep my sight on him. Mama warned me before leaving the house to be careful. As soon as I saw the exit sign, I hurried up and scurried out the building."

"We will look into this."

Leon and Jill left the police station. Leon and Jill arrived home. Eric and Rose ran to the car. Leon carried a box of pizza in his hand.

"Pizza again! We are going to turn into a huge pizza," said Eric, with a huge smile on his face.

"Yep, pizzas, with pepperoni!"

Paint the Town Red

WEDNESDAY SHOPPED TILL SHE DROPPED on Friday. Wednesday found the perfect red outfit for her hot date with Det. Ted Swoop at Bloomingdale's. To complete the look, Wednesday went to the MAC makeup counter for their glamour makeover. MAC got wise to the girls who just went to the makeup counter to have their faces made up for special occasions. Now they force you to purchase at least forty dollars in makeup products.

Wednesday sat in the tall high chair. She observed a number of women standing around the makeup. People watched the transformation of her face. "Is this a special event?"

"Yes, I am going on a hot date. I have to dazzle him."

"What colors are you wearing?"

"I am going to wear red."

The makeup artist advised Wednesday, "Berry would make your lips pop. "I'm not trying to come on to you but you have beautiful lips."

"Let me see, I think this makeup color will look fabulous on your face, Wednesday. To highlight your hazel eye color, mmm…let me see. Girl, you will look fabulous in smoky shades of brown."

Wednesday engaged in a few lines of conversation during the transformation.

"How long have you been in the business?"

"I have been in the business for sixteen years. Oh I am so sorry; my name is Manny. I do private makeovers too.

That was so rude of me."

"Manny, that's okay."

Manny said, "Wednesday today is your lucky day. Wednesday that today is her lucky day. With the purchase of $50.00 worth of MAC products, customers receive a free cosmetic gift bag. You're gonna love what's inside. There are at least ten different shades of lipstick."

Manny handed Wednesday the gift bag while putting the finishing touches on her face. Wednesday eagerly opened each tube of lipstick. Much to her chagrin at least eight shades were muted, dull, or definitely did not match her African-American skin tone.

"I'm high-yellow. These invisible shades of color do not highlight my luscious lips."

Wednesday bust out in laughter. "I just knew I finally arrived in lipstick heaven—only to be disappointed with the colors."

"Enjoy your date Wednesday."

A Dream Fulfilled

DET. SWOOP ARRIVED AT WEDNESDAY's house for their first date. Det. Swoop did not at all look like a man in his late fifties. He looked like he was in his early forties. He wore a white linen pantsuit. The white set off his beautiful brown skin tone, his burly muscular body and his wavy short black hair. Ted escorted Wednesday to his fully loaded Escalade. He eagerly opened the car door for her. "You look exquisite in that red dress and red shoes." He could hardly take his eyes off of her. He turned on the radio and opened up the electronic moon roof. "Did you grow up in New York?"

"No, Ted, I grew up in Mt. Hope, a small town in New York. I moved to New Jersey because the rents were cheaper, but I'm ready to move on."

"You can come live with me." Ted laughed.

"After graduating from the University of Hartford's undergraduate Mass Communications program, I worked as a salesgirl at Abraham & Straus. I wanted to be a buyer. After one year of working in the women's handbags and accessories department, I decided to attend the Fashion Institute of Technology, said Wednesday.

"As a high school student, I took a course in sewing and made many of the clothes I wore. I received compliments on the clothes that I made."

"I wanted to become a prominent buyer in a department store. After submitting a few resumes, I received an invite to participate in a group interview for a position in a major department store's buyer's training program. Boy was I nervous. This young white guy sat next to me. He struck up a conversation with me, a conversation that led to him saying, 'You'll get this job. You're black.' I remember saying 'Not necessarily.' Guess what, Ted? I did not get the job."

"Retail never fit my pocket. My bag was too big for the retail dollar, Ted."

"You do have a way with word."

"Ted that's not the worst thing that happened to me in retail. I tell you. Wednesday shook her head. Retail has a way of tickling my soul but rattling my nerves. I got mad with Abraham & Straus. You see, Ted, they promoted a lady in the department to a supervisory position over me because she did not have an undergraduate degree. I had a degree. I was so naive. The color of my skin did not enter my mind. I just knew she did not have the same educational credentials that I have. I suppose that was my first introduction into the many injustices that we often face."

"I figured I would work in the department store for a number of years and in time, become the sole proprietor of my own clothing store. I took a few business courses at a college and realized that I found a niche in advertising and marketing. As a student in fashion design, I majored in designing women's apparel. I like working with leather."

"Can you design a leather coat for me to wear in the fall?"

"I think I can. I'll design a sketch, show it to you, and if you like the design. I will create it for you."

"I can't wait to see the design, Wednesday."

Ted pulled into an outside parking spot located right next to the pier. A crowd of people gathered at the ticket booth. Wednesday noticed a number of women staring at Ted.

"Ted, what prompted you to go into law enforcement?"

"Call it fate, I suppose. Someone suggested that I take the police officer exam. I graduated from college but found it difficult to locate a job. I scored in the high nineties. I was one of the first to be called for a position as a NYC police officer. As the years passed, I realized that I thoroughly enjoyed the impromptu action afforded to me in the police department. No two days are alike. Yes, it is dangerous to walk a beat, but investigating crime scenes is intriguing. It's much like trying to place the pieces of a jigsaw puzzle together. As a child, I always enjoyed putting jigsaw puzzles together."

Wednesday laughed. "Sounds like you have a large inner child inside of you."

"I suppose that is a good way of describing it," said Ted. "Well Ted, my fresh out of school career goals never got off the ground. Today, I am a painter and amateur photographer. Some of my photography was featured in a photo contest. I won first prize."

When I was offered a job at Omari Boutique, I was excited. This is my 'meantime' job. A few of my art pieces were displayed in the store. That's how I got to know Omari and Susan.

"I had just been laid off from Abraham and Straus, so I jumped at the employment offer. Omari's going to exhibit some of my photography too. I'll invite you to the exhibit. Most of my photos feature nature shots. The problem with me is I have so many things on my plate that I bounce from one thing to another.

"So, Ted, what dreams do you have?"

"I want to open a private investigation firm."

"That's fabulous, Ted. I am a firm believer that the one who shoots for the moon may not make it fully to the moon but they might land in Jupiter."

Ted laughed. "You have a way with words."

"Now it's up to you, Ted, to find out if the moon is closer than Jupiter."

"In this case, you must specify what moon you speak of. There are two moons flying round on Jupiter, and baby I'd fly with you to the farthest moon."

Wednesday laughed so hard her stomach hurt.

"No, for real, I'll fly you to the moon if you want me to."

Wednesday blushed.

"Where did you grow up, Ted?"

"In Harlem, but my family is originally from California. I spent many summers in California. Have you toured California, it's a beautiful state?"

"Yes, I have been to the San Francisco Bay Area. Sausalito is a beautiful area. The drive down the coast was awesome."

A loud baritone voice from the public announcement system interrupted their conversation: "We're boarding now for the Sunset Smooth Jazz cruise. Welcome aboard!"

Ted and Wednesday were among the first to board the boat. They decided to sit close to the band. Ted and Wednesday prepared a plate from the ship's lavish buffet. The night was gorgeous. The star covered sky was clear. Ted ordered a round of drinks. Wednesday ordered a rum and coke, and Ted ordered Jack Daniels. After eating, Ted and Wednesday walked to the top level of the yacht. The view was awesome. They marveled at the wonderful NYC skyline. As they cruised down the Hudson, the ship's on-board narrator pointed out notable buildings. Within twenty minutes of departure from Chelsea Pier, Will Downing opened his set with "Something Special."

Ted did not disclose to Wednesday that he had a personal connection to Will Downing. He phoned Will Downing's music manager shortly before the event and requested that Downing sing a song to Wednesday. Ted gently eased his hand into her hand. Will Downing set the stage for a lifetime of love between Ted and Wednesday. It was up to them to keep the flame lit.

Will Downing's musical set ended with "After Tonight." After a round of applause, Downing came back on to the stage and, as they say in show biz, he brought the curtain down with "Test of Time." Many stood up and moved to the beat of this up-tempo song. The boat pulled into the dock as Downing sang his final song. Wednesday obtained Will Downing's business card before leaving the ship.

Ted drove Wednesday to her apartment in Newark. Prior to Wednesday's departure from the car, Ted thanked Wednesday.

"Thank you for what?"

"I thoroughly enjoyed our time together and look forward to spending many days and nights with you."

Wednesday thought, *Oh how sweet. Seems like a perfect gentleman to me.* Wednesday told Ted to her call when he arrived home. Wednesday kissed him softly on his cheek.

As she was about to leave, Ted grabbed her gently around her waist and kissed her passionately on her lips.

"Good night Wednesday, sleep tight. You really are something special."

Det. Swoop drove back home to Harlem with a huge smile on his face. Ted just completed renovations on his 128th Street brownstone. Det. Swoop sensed that Harlem was about to go through a renaissance, so he purchased prime property in Harlem at public auctions before the real estate market sizzled. The presence of dog walkers in Harlem did not existent ten years ago. Many whites moved uptown to Harlem.

Det. Swoop unlocked the door and immediately took his shoes off in the vestibule. He did not want to dirty the off cream carpet. When Det. Swoop purchased the brownstone, he toyed with the idea of leaving the bare wood floors exposed but decided against doing so. He loved the feel of a warm blanket of carpet underneath his bare feet in the morning. Det. Swoop phoned Wednesday to let her know he was home. He was wide awake. Det. Swoop opened his mail and checked his e-mail. Suddenly, a thought came to his mind regarding the fake paintings.

Det. Swoop called a source in Nigeria. After a lengthy discussion it was determined that the paintings were indeed being shipped from Africa. Some of Det. Swoop's best detective work was completed in the wee hours of the morning. He could not wait to tell Summerlyn about his findings.

Swoop advised Chief Summerlyn, "based on preliminary information obtained from the investigation. I need to travel to Nigeria to continue the investigation. Those paintings were imported from Africa."

Chief Summerlyn responded, "That is truly amazing—"
"Even I know that stolen art is usually taken from Italy."

"Nigerians recognize the value in African-American art."

Within minutes, Chief Summerlyn made a few phone calls. A round-trip airplane ticket and hotel reservations were ordered for Det. Swoop and Newman.

"Your flight to Nigeria is scheduled to leave on Monday at 6:00 a.m."

Det. Swoop was not exactly anxious to go to Africa. He immediately thought about his lovely date with Wednesday. He hoped to see her soon. He went to bed with warm thoughts of Wednesday.

He also woke up with warm thoughts of Wednesday, and it showed. Det. Swoop rolled out the bed and ran into the cold shower. Det. Swoop called Wednesday at the boutique around eleven.

"You know, that home cooked meal you promised to cook me is on my mind. I was hoping we could get together sometime this week, but I have to go overseas on a business trip. I'll call you when I return, Wednesday."

Wednesday responded, "Don't worry. The dinner date offer can wait until you return. Ciao!"

The private cab company arrived on time for Det. Swoop's trip to Kennedy Airport. The streets were empty, so the drive to Kennedy was quick. He traveled to Africa before, so he was somewhat aware of the nuances and the underground crime network in Nigeria. Newman met Swoop at the airport.

Det. Ted Swoop already researched the various art galleries in the area. Det. Swoop and Newman slept during much of the flight. When awake, he read a novel and reviewed the business section of *The New York Times*.

"Ladies and gentlemen, please secure all your belongings and fasten your seat belts. The plane will land in Nigeria in twenty minutes. The current temperature in Nigeria is 70 degrees. Thank you for flying with us."

The uneventful landing in Nigeria jolted Swoop and Newman awake placing. A cab awaited their arrival in the baggage claim area. They were driven to the Nigerian Hilton. After washing up, Det. Swoop and Newman began the chore of visiting a number of galleries. They rented a car on a daily basis. With the high price of gas, they decided to go with an economy-class car. That way they could ease in and out of traffic.

Det. Swoop and Newman arrived at the first gallery. He noticed nothing unusual. The gallery did not carry Afrocentric paintings. They traveled to two more galleries, and again, everything appeared fine. Their fourth stop at a gallery presented him with the information he needed. There were two similar paintings aligned on the wall of the gallery in Nigeria that were displayed at Omari Boutique. Duplication of numbers could clearly be seen. Det. Swoop and Newman immediately left the gallery. They proceeded to the nearest police station. Det. Swoop called Summerlyn.

"Bingo! We found the gallery. The duplicate paintings are located at the Nigerian Connection gallery in Nigeria. There is only one gallery on this strip."

Chief Summerlyn was aware of Det. Swoop's abilities and did not question his findings. "Ted, the paintings are rare. This guy is a famous African-American artist. There are only two original paintings in the series."

The Nigerian police will proceed with the investigation, interrogation and ultimate arrest of the criminals when apprehended.

"After the interrogation, I am sure that we will have more information. The Nigerian police will notify you if they need help. They realize we want this wrapped up in a matter of days. "Of course you and Newman will have to follow-up on the leads in the states."

"Okay, Chief."

"Det. Swoop and Newman, we expect you to return within the next two weeks."

Chief Summerlyn spoke to the commanding officer in Nigeria. This was not the first time he had requested support from him. Chief Akiboh was always cooperative. His department was highly qualified to proceed with the investigation. Previous investigative requests were handled with care and proficiency.

Chief Akiboh was given all of the information and advised of the details. He assigned a team of police and ordered a surveillance team. The team immediately examined the layout of the gallery. A few plainclothes police posing as clients nonchalantly examined the gallery's video surveillance system. Undercover cops were instructed to pose as customers, browse the collection, and purchase some of the counterfeited paintings.

The first officer arrived at the crowded gallery and purchased one of the paintings. Another officer arrived at the gallery within a week and also purchased the same painting. Additional officers including Det. Newman and Swoop who are fluent in Yoruba arrived at the gallery within a week. Newman purchased the same painting. That particular purchase sealed the case. Only two paintings had been produced, but there were three paintings available for purchase. Obviously one was a counterfeit copy. The plainclothes officer reached into his pocket and quickly showed his gold shield to the clerk. The officer observed the Nigerian female clerk, who appeared to be in her early twenties, placing her hand underneath the counter. She observed a few opportunistic patrons scurrying out the door with an expensive painting or two. They did not get far. The police were waiting outside. Sensing that there was probably a silent alert signal to someone unseen, the officer pushed a silent alert to his team and brandished his shield around the room. A team of undercover cops swiftly entered into the gallery.

Undercover officers were already in the gallery and were dispersed into various areas in the gallery. Two burly men walked into the showroom. One man immediately fired a round from his gun. Pandemonium broke out. People screamed some ducked and hid, while some patrons ran toward the exit door. A strong wave of legs could be seen fleeing to the door. Some pushed. One person nearly got crushed during the fiasco, however, he managed to escape unscathed. A few patrons heard the sound of gunfire ring out in the gallery.

Frightened patrons did not look back, for fear of what they might see. The smoke, cleared. Two men and the female clerk were slain. The second man, identified as one of the owners of the boutique, hung onto a thin veil of breath. He barely managed to whisper, "Help…"

Officers found him bleeding profusely. He was slumped over a desk in the showroom. His last breath of air was breathed when he was placed on the gurney and wheeled out of the gallery. A final gasp of air could be heard and then his buxom body went limp. His arm fell from his waist downward to the ground. Due to the fast actions of the undercover officers, the majority of the patrons and staff escaped a potential massacre. The team of police confiscated and seized all written documents in the gallery. The gallery's computers were confiscated. It would take a number of weeks before the police could scour through all the files.

The street was closed off immediately. A number of helicopters flew overhead. One could see the police officer leaning out the helicopter with a telescopic riffle in hand. Police cars swarmed like ants on the ground. The injured bodies were placed in the ambulances. The bullet-ridden bodies were identified by individuals who resided in the area. Swoop and Newman escaped unscathed and quickly phoned Summerlyn.

"Great work! Now you can return home. I'll see you in 48 hours. I have a team here who will remain in contact with the Nigerian police."

Paramedics immediately pronounced all of them dead at the scene of the crime. A large crowd of people gathered at the end of the police tape. Flashing cameras signified that the reporters arrived at the crime scene. Reporters with well-known names were prevented from interviewing the police men. No one was allowed to enter the gallery, except those who assisted in the investigation and recovery of evidence, and the forensics examiners.

During their search of the premises, they located a key. After several attempts to use the key to unlock various doors in the gallery, they finally located a small metal box. The key fit perfectly in the box. A forensics expert with gloves on his hands finally unlocked the green metal box. Inside the box was a list. An encrypted list that could not be decrypted without the help of a team of expert cryptanalysts, therefore, they consulted with an expert cryptanalyst. The mere fact that the information was completed in a code signified that the information contained in the small metal box might unravel the mystery. Modern-day technology has led to the invention of powerful computers used to analyze cypher-text.

Unexpected Delivery

TED SWOOP'S MOTHER DIED TWO years ago from heart disease. She was also diagnosed with Alzheimer's. He was not prepared for Alzheimer's, even though he knew many people who suffered with the disease. Swoop managed to stay above water but was relieved when his mother passed. She was no longer the vibrant person that she once was. Watching her suffer was difficult. He could see clearly that she was trying to fight a battle that just was not going to be won.

Swoop always enjoyed the company of the elderly. He hated crimes against the elderly. When he received cases of this type he put his heart and soul into the investigation. Det. Swoop's birth was unexpected and unplanned. His mother was thirty-eight years old when she gave birth to him. Back in the day, that was considered to be old. He was always around older people. He knew when to speak and was trained to "stay out of grown folks' conversations."

He often played in his room with his toys when his parents' friends visited. Theirs was an open house; every weekend there was company. The phone rang.

"Hey Swoop, this is Wednesday. How have you been?"

"Wednesday, I am so wrapped up in this case, but I have not forgotten about you. I will call you later in the week. It would be good for us to get together and spend some quality time together."

Det. Swoop heard a beep, indicating that another call was coming in. "Wednesday, I have to go. I think this might be a call on the case."

"Okay, Ted, you take care—"

Det. Swoop blew a kiss into the phone and then clicked to the next call. Swoop's sixth sense told him it was his chief.

"They found an encrypted message that needs to be decoded. We should have the results in a matter of days. I think they will find detailed information on this."

"We'll see."

"The records revealed that somehow this theft is tied to Omari Boutique. "I kind of figured that."

"We need you to investigate all the employees at the boutique. We know that Omari Boutique has grown substantially. He recently opened a perfume line. Look into that. If you can pinpoint the timetable, I am sure that will be helpful in solving the crime."

"The Omari perfume line In the Wind just opened within the past month, so it seems highly unlikely that anyone in the line was involved. Right now it truly does not appear that any of the direct line staff at the boutique are involved."

Swoop informed his chief that he needed to recluse himself from investigating. I fell in love with one of the employees, Wednesday. "I went on a date with her recently, and I really enjoy her company."

"I'll ask another officer to look into her background. As you know, you are not to talk to Wednesday about this case. In fact, it's best that you put that on hold."

"Wait a minute, Chief. You can't infringe upon my personal life. Tell you what, sir I'll excuse myself from the entire case."

"No, Swoop, we need you to assist on this investigation, but at this point I'll have to re-assign you to another case. Det. Swoop you are temporarily reassigned to another case until we can complete the investigation on all employees of Omari Boutique."

"Okay. Look, you know I am a professional. I know I can complete this investigation and not jeopardize my career or personal relationship with Wednesday. Your first idea works. Have someone else look into her background, but please do it quickly, sir."

Swoop phoned Omari and obtained a full roster of the staff. The Omari Boutique, LLC quietly grew to a staff of fifty. This included their subsidiary company of Omari Boutique, In the Wind perfume.

There were various departments, including mail order, stock, and of course, the administrative staff that needed to be investigated. Swoop sat down with Omari and discussed the hiring dates of each member of the staff. Swoop, with Omari's help, was able to pin down the timetable. It seemed that the incident occurred eight weeks ago.

As per Omari's personnel files, a gentleman in the warehouse joined the company exactly eight weeks ago. Det. Swoop gathered the names and addresses of the employees. Omari was advised not to discuss the case with anyone. Det. Swoop returned to the police station, where he completed a preliminary background check on the employees. Officer Hammond ran the background check on Wednesday. He arranged an appointment time whereby he could interview her. In the interest of fairness, Wednesday was the first employee to be interviewed.

Summerlyn summoned Det. Swoop into his office. "Is this quick enough for you?"

Within three days, the police department reviewed Wednesday's background check and called her into the office for an interview. Wednesday's background check was clean as a whistle. She would not be placed on the suspect list. Swoop was relieved.

"Don't forget to invite me to the wedding, Det. Swoop." Summerlyn smiled and left the room.

Swoop reached into his pocket and pulled his cell phone out his pocket to check the text messages that recently came in. He immediately called Wednesday.

"Hey, baby, I missed you. Summerlyn wanted me to interview all staff of Omari Boutique, but once I disclosed that you and I have a personal relationship, I was forced to recuse myself from the case so to speak. I suppose you realize that I was forbidden to contact you because of the investigation."

"I assumed it had to do with the investigation, Ted. We need not talk about the investigation. There's a gospel concert at my church on Sunday, I would like you to come."

"Wednesday, that sounds great. I can pick you up. What time is the concert?"

"Great! The concert is at Genesis I Baptist Church in Mount Hope, NY. The doors open at 6 p.m. The concert begins at 8:00 p.m. They hired one of those gospel stars to perform at the church fundraiser. Do come prepared to give. They often collect a free-will offering. We are desperately in need of a new boiler and roof."

"Lord knows I need God in my life. Every day, I get on my knees and pray that I will wake up to see the next day unharmed. I carry God in my left pocket every day near my heart."

"Wednesday, you travel there every Sunday?"

"Yes, I grew up in that church. I remember when that church was half the size that it is now. I remember things that most of the current parishioners can't remember."

Ted laughed. "You should become the church historian. Omari sings in the choir too, Wednesday. Omari goes wherever the Holy Spirit leads him."

"He came to church one Sunday, and he stuck up a friendly conversation with me. He was the featured soloist. That's how I met him."

"I can't wait to hear you sing in the choir, Wednesday. I have to go to work now, Wednesday. Talk to you later."

Swoop returned to the police station and completed a background check on the employees. Almar Javier's background presented an interesting picture. He was hired eight weeks ago. Almar Javier, a black-Hispanic, was born in the late seventies. Javier graduated from a Bronx high school. A background check revealed that he had one misdemeanor for criminal trespassing, but the record was sealed. The charge was dismissed. His work attendance record was a bit shaky. Some employees advised the supervisor that they observed Javier with reddened eyes and slurred speech. Supervisors began to notice the smell of alcohol on his breath.

Swoop made a surprise visit to the warehouse where Almar was employed. Almar was slovenly dressed in blue jeans and a ripped T-shirt. His eyes appeared to be red. Swoop identified himself as the police. Almar was interviewed in a small office room at the warehouse. The warehouse shipped In The Wind perfume to various distributors and retail shops. He appeared to be nervous.

His brow was sweaty, and he was somewhat jittery. His speech was slurred, and at times he seemed to be tongue-tied. Det. Swoop terminated the interview when he was dispatched back to the headquarters. Det. Swoop sensed that something was wrong.

Sometimes the best course of action is to sit and wait.

A couple of days later, the warehouse manager called Omari.

"We caught Almar taking one painting out of a crate and replacing it with another painting. The painting that he took out of the sealed crate were contained in a tubular carrier. Almar quickly placed some of expensive paintings in the carriers and shifted into a corner of the warehouse."

Almar's station was located near the warehouse door, a door that led to the loading dock.

"It was very easy for Almar to place the paintings with lesser value onto the belt. There were only two other workers who worked in the warehouse on that day. When the exchange was completed, no one was in the warehouse. Almar quickly stamped an invisible code on the crate. We caught it all on camera."

Omari phoned Swoop. "They caught Almar— on camera. Almar was switching paintings." Det. Swoop dropped everything. "I'm coming to the store. I want to see that video. I'll be there in less than twenty minutes." Det. Swoop reviewed the tape in the presence of Omari.

"We have enough evidence to arrest this guy." Swoop and his partners arrived at the Omari warehouse. Almar was there. Almar sensed something was wrong. As soon as Almar spotted Swoop, he tried to run. Fortunately, most of the workers were gone for the day. The floor was relatively empty.

Swoop shouted, "Halt! You are under arrest." Almar dug into his pocket and brandished a knife.

"Drop that, or we will shoot."

Almar lunged toward Det. Swoop with the knife. Swoop wasted no time firing his gun. He purposefully aimed to maim, not to kill Almar. It was obvious that Almar was a key figure in the crime. The police needed him to survive. A loud pop exploded from the gun. The bullet struck him in his leg. Almar screamed in pain and fell onto the ground. Blood spilled onto the cement floor.

An ambulance was dispatched Paramedics stabilized him and placed him on the stretcher. The police read him his rights. He was immediately placed him under arrest.

Chief Summerlyn arrived at the warehouse. "Good job," said Chief Summerlyn. "Make sure you write your report immediately Swoop."

After a week in the hospital, Almar eventually agreed to admit to his involvement in a professional art theft ring. He gave a written statement to the police. He was the mastermind of the entire smuggling ring. He was thirty-seven years old. He lived like a pauper, so no one knew he was a millionaire criminal. He traveled to Mexico on a regular basis. His twenty-two-thousand-square-foot mansion contained a horse farm and in-ground swimming pool.

Almar's mistake was that he had not done an in-house art theft in a number of years and was rusty. As Almar's empire grew, he employed others to get their hands dirty. Omari's observations and immediate notification to the police thwarted the crime. This time, perhaps out of sheer boredom, Almar had decided to be on the front line. A different type of mud is flung in the face of those on the front line.

He planned the theft of the paintings for months. His first task was to become gainfully employed at the boutique. The crime would have remained unnoticed if not for the video camera.

Almar recovered from his wound. Within five days, he was transferred to the federal prison. His lengthy trial resulted in a guilty verdict. Almar's sworn written statement was clear. The evidence proved the case. Even Almar's lawyer said, "You can't win this case."

Few visitors visited him during his hospitalization. He stared excessively at the window. Because of his fixation on the window and apparent depression, the hospital psychiatrist ordered a suicide watch.

Almar Javier admitted his involvement in a Mexican drug cartel. Almar's sworn written statement sealed the case. He was sentenced to twenty-five years in federal prison. Almar provided a number of leads to the authorities in exchange for a lighter sentence.

Fifteen men associated with the ring were arrested. The ring had a number of stations in various countries throughout the world. Their clientele was extensive. Their operation also catered to the needs of a number of high-ranking statesmen and rich private investors. Bootleg art that could be sold for a handsome profit in the underground world. The encrypted message found at the gallery in Africa was finally decoded. The message contained a list of stolen paintings and the locations of the places of the heist.

Javier's art napping ring was massive. He was a mid-level member of the ring. He hit a number of galleries. Javier's gang actually surpassed Martin Cahill's record of having the second largest art theft case in history. He stole over sixty million dollars in art.

The theft that Javier planned at Omari Boutique was a minor theft compared to other art studios and museums he had stolen from in the past.

Chief Summerlyn's unit won another award for its outstanding work in handling this art napping case. Det. Swoop received a promotion and special recognition for resolving the case expeditiously. He was elevated to the position of Assistant Police Chief. Det. Swoop remained in that position until he resigned to start his own investigations company.

Wednesday was a godsend to Det. Swoop. "She is the only woman in my life who totally calms me down. She listens to my dreams and encourages me to turn my dreams into reality."

Wednesday had a colorful love history until, as she states, "God struck me down, and AIDS became a major threat to all." Jumping in the bed right away was no longer a way of life.

"Thank God that was a short-lived lifestyle, Wednesday, you're special."

Det. Swoop was intrigued by Wednesday's high level of social consciousness and earnest desire to assist the needy. Det. Swoop knew right away that Wednesday was a good-hearted person. Det. Swoop always said, "Animals and kids do not lie. They have extraordinary senses." Wednesday's love for art was cultivated and accepted by Samuel. She continued to sow her seeds in art. Her artistic talents fast became known to many. In support of Wednesday's creative ramblings, Ted converted one of the apartments in the brownstone into an art studio.

Wednesday had contracts at various companies, but her bread and butter came from the contract that she had with Omari Boutique. Her part-time position at Omari Boutique provided her with a wealth of experience and lead to an increase Wednesday's art sales. Wednesday's art collection consisted of collages on canvass with various odd pieces pasted on canvas. She was also a nature photographer. Omari Boutique sizzled with excitement. Every artist dreamed about displaying their creative designs at the Boutique. Omari Boutique became the new African-American art gallery of choice.

Within six months of meeting Wednesday, Swoop proposed to her. He purchased a one-carat diamond of superior quality from a company in South Africa. He was able to locate a flawless round diamond with excellent clarity. He shipped the diamond to a well-known jeweler so that the diamond could be set in a beautiful band. They embedded the diamond in a simple, twisted diamond band with small diamond chips.

The engagement band also had a matching wedding ring made of diamonds. It was a classic ring that would remain fashionable throughout the years. Ted and Wednesday married at Wednesday's childhood church, Genesis I Baptist Church in Mount Hope, New York. The sermon was performed by the "celebrity" minister. The pews were decorated with exotic white orchids.

The large wedding party consisted of eight bridesmaids, who wore purple. Wednesday's best friend, Ann, was the maid of honor. Wednesday's dress was elegant. The drop waist own formed a V that fell just below her navel. It was exquisite. The beaded bodice contained sequins. The bottom of the satin gown featured a cathedral-length train that glided with ease on the floor. It was awesome. It showed off her well-shaped behind—and fit perfectly on her size 18 body and showed off all her curves.

Wednesday's long locks cascaded down the side of her face. She wore a perfectly placed elegant hairpiece in her hair. She was sexy yet angelic. The berry colored lipstick sizzled.

Her hand held bouquet featured shades of purple, pink, and white. Wednesday recited a portion of her poem to Ted, "Love is winter stripped bare. You are my love, my life, and reason for living. With this ring I do wed."

The reception for two hundred people was held at the Bronx Botanical Gardens. A rare appearance by James Mtume and his famous saxophonist father Jimmy Heath at the reception lead to an impromptu jam session. Everyone got up when Mtume played Juicy Fruit. This lavish reception was well attended by close friends and associates of the bride and groom. Bob Slade was the best man in the wedding party.

After the reception, a horse-drawn carriage drove Wednesday and Ted around the park. They left the gardens in a limousine that drove them down the somewhat crowded West Side Highway to the piers. The limousine arrived at the piers. They unloaded their designer luggage and boarded the *Carnival Victory* cruise ship. A band standing just outside of the boat ramp welcomed and cheered the newlyweds. Each registered newlywed received a special gift upon entering the boat.

Their seven-day cruise included stops in Miami, San Juan, Puerto Rico, Saint Thomas, and Saint Maarten. This was the night that they would finally unleash their love upon each other. Wednesday and Ted enjoyed the trade winds of Saint Thomas the most. During their brief stay on the island, they managed to attend a timeshare seminar. They decided to purchase a two-bedroom duplex waterfront unit. They briefly shopped in Charlotte Amelia, the well-known shopping area in Saint Thomas. Ted purchased a pair of diamonds for Wednesday. Wednesday purchased a Breitling Bentley Mark VI watch for her husband.

The newlyweds enjoyed a luscious wedding night. Rose petals, champagne and bubble lead to an intimate night of love on the sea.

Upon returning to the States, Ted and Wednesday noticed that there were a number of messages left on their respective business phones. Both agreed not to listen to any of the messages until they returned home. In fact, they clearly indicated that they would not return any phone calls until their honeymoon was over.

"Sorry, we are unable to answer your call. We are on our honeymoon and will not return until Friday."

A flood of messages congratulating them on their recent nuptials filled their respective voice mail. The first call Ted received was from his former chief.

Ted returned the call immediately. Chief Summerlyn advised that his department received an anonymous tip on an old case that was never resolved.

The chief asked Ted if he remembered the shooting of Pention.

Summerlyn said, "How could I possibly forget?"

Few of the cases in the Summerlyn unit remained unsolved, but that particular case stumped the entire squad. Unlike many of the cases he encountered, all evidence yielded negative results and findings. Det. Swoop knew it was going to be a difficult case to solve, but he did not remember the intimate details of the case.

"Oh, I remember, Pention. He was the street hustler who also dabbled in drugs."

"Yes, that's the right case." The chief advised that he wanted to set up a conference with Ted as soon as possible.

"How does tomorrow at noon fit into your schedule, Ted?"

"Well, I planned on taking tomorrow off, but since this case has been outstanding for two years, I have no qualms with meeting you tomorrow."

"Okay, I'll come into your office, Ted. It is always nice to get away from headquarters. You just make sure that your lovely wife cooks a nice lunch so we can chow down together. She is truly a wonderful cook, Ted. Last time I visited you she cooked fried chicken and potato salad. Her homemade sweet potato pie was slamming."

"Yes, Mrs. Swoop is a mighty fine everything. "Ted laughed and whispered in Summerlyn's ear because Wednesday was in earshot, "She is sexy in bed too."

Summerlyn laughed. "Congratulations! You two are no longer virgins to each other. You finally popped that cherry. I'll see you tomorrow, Ted."

Summerlyn arrived at Ted's Total Care Investigation Agency. The traffic was lean, so he was able to sail through it with ease. Summerlyn gained a substantial amount of weight. He rolled out of his car with a leather briefcase that contained important leads and information on the case.

"Welcome, Summerlyn. Have a seat in the conference room." Det. Swoop purchased the cherry-wood conference table at an office warehouse's going out of business sale for a fraction of its original cost.

The trail of papers was long, but the two of them were able to narrow down the documents to fifty. Summerlyn informed Det. Swoop that the investigation was reopened because the station received an anonymous tip.

"I hate to have unsolved cases on my watch."

Summerlyn filled Swoop in on what happened.

A lady with an Irish brogue phoned the station. "Officer, I observed three men standing in the area on the night of the murder. One guy was black. He appeared to be in his mid-forties. He was light-skinned and muscular. One could easily see he has a yearly membership in a fitness club. From a distance he appeared to be approximately six inches tall. The other was Hispanic. He appeared to be in his thirties, approximately five feet tall and thin. The third person was white. He had dark brown hair. He appeared to be in his—let me think. I believe he was in his early forties. He wore a heart-shaped tattoo on his upper left arm. There was an inscription written underneath the heart."

"What was the inscription?"

"The guy was too far away from me to see the lettering on his arm."

"May I have your name—?"

There was a sudden hang-up and then the sound of a dial tone rang in the ear of the officer. The call could not be traced. The unidentified female had phoned the police station from an unlisted phone number.

"Ted, I know this is very limited information, but with these documents, you just might be able to crack this crime." "Okay, Summerlyn. I'll scratch my head and comb through these documents. In addition, I would like to have access to the original fibers file."

"Not a problem, Det. Swoop. If you are able to complete this investigation and locate the assailants, our department will pay you $19,000 in addition to your regular hourly rate. I know that's low, but you know we are in a recession."

"Summerlyn, why don't you just throw in the thousand, make it an even $20,000 and it's a deal? I know that department. You got money. You guys are cheap," said Det. Swoop.

"Det. Swoop, it's a deal. Now if for some reason you are unable to resolve the crime, we will give you $5,000 minus the hourly rate…that is what you charge right? According to this pay schedule you charge $70.00 per hour."

"That is correct."

"I'll put together an independent sub-contractor contract and have it ready for you tomorrow, Det. Swoop. We are willing to give you three months to resolve the crime."

"I'll call you within the week to see how much progress you have made. If you need me in the interim, call me Ted."

Ted spent much of the night combing through the documents. One document in particular stood out. Pention's autopsy report indicated that the angle of the wound indicated that it was an upper right-hand jab into Pention's gut with a knife that killed Pention. Pention's body immediately filled with blood; a main artery had been punctured. He drowned in his own blood. The blunt object hit to the side of his head seemed to have been the beginning of the fight. It seemed that the gunshot was just a final dramatization of the violent nature of the killer. Neighbors reported hearing a loud scream and then the loud pop, a sound that was heard too often in the hood.

A review of mug shots that matched the description given to the police was ordered. A few matched the description given. Ted reviewed their criminal history and weeded out a few names. He placed a phone call to another eyewitness.

"Hi Sade, this is Investigator Swoop. I need you to come into the office."

Sade, a retired postal clerk, who appeared to about fifty-eight years old spoke with a strong West Indian accent.

When Sade came into his office, Det. Swoop pulled out a number of mug shots. "Any of these photos resemble the man?"

The lady said, "I told you I did not get a clear look but this guy here looks familiar. I have seen him in the neighborhood. From a distance, I can see how he fits the body type of the man who I saw. He also has a tattoo on his arm with a heart."

The man she picked out had a criminal record that included numerous arrests for selling illegal drugs. He was involved in a shooting about two months ago. Two other men were with him. He was identified as the trigger man. Rumor had it he went underground to escape arrest.

"Det. Swoop, his name is Joey Junga. He lived right around the corner in a brick building that was badly in need of repair. I know he sold marijuana in the neighborhood, but he could have sold other drugs too. Sometimes cars parked in front of the building. People ran in and out of that building like flies swarming around an open plate of food. He must have some good stuff too, because cars with out-of-state plates often arrived. I'm talking' fancy as all get out. Cadillacs, Mercedes Benz—the list was long. You name it, it was there. There was a fashion show of cars parading around, some with convertible tops driving up the block to cop some drugs."

"Thank you, Sade, you have been very helpful."

Det. Swoop drove to the neighborhood looking for a man that fit the description of Joey. He went to the building where Joey lived.

"Is Joey here? Someone told me he's got the good stuff. I need a G of coke."

"Man, he's not here. What you want?" Det. Swoop observed a number of patrons purchasing heroin, crack and cocaine. Det. Swoop purchased a bag of weed and a G of cocaine and left. Ted immediately phoned Summerlyn.

"Hey Summerlyn, I found the spot. They are selling drugs there. I need backup. I'm at 922 Prospect Avenue, Bronx, New York. The spot is located on the fourth floor in a walkup building. It's a poorly lit building. You can't miss it. Steady stream of people coming in and out of here."

Det. Swoop handed the officer the bag of weed and coke that he purchased.

Swoop spoke into his body microphone. It was wired to the police station. "Something is wrong," screamed Swoop. I just heard multiple rounds of gun shots.

"Come fast, I need back-up. Newman was not assigned to this case. I just heard gunshots—call the ambulance."

Four squad cars arrived within minutes. Screams could be heard from the street. The cops jumped out of their cars and ran into the building with guns drawn. The officers observed one man attempting to climb out of the fourth floor window. He ultimately fell from the window. One man slumped on the stairs, coughed up blood, and screamed in pain. He was shot in the chest. In between screams, he managed to point out the shooter. He pointed out Joey Junga.

They placed him on a stretcher and wheeled him into the ambulance. "I owed him money I owed h—" He was unable to finish the sentence. He lost consciousness.

The police station received an anonymous call stating that the other two men involved in the murder were among those who they just arrested.

"What's your name?"

The man hung up the phone, but just before hanging up the caller said, "Meet me on the corner of Prospect Avenue and Kelly Street. I'll point the other two out to you."

A plainclothes officer met him at the corner. The plainclothes officer approached him with caution. Immediately upon seeing his face, he knew he worked with him on another situation.

"I know you—you are Johnny Morebetter." Morebetter nodded his head yes. Morebetter who was known on the street for pimping, informed the officers that he came forward because one of those men beat up his girl.

"I might not be on the straight and narrow, but I'm not physically abusive to women."

He pointed out the two men. They did not pull the trigger. Joey was bragging about killing some man named Pention. He gave the guys a high five and walked away so as not to bring attention himself.

Meanwhile, across the street, Joey Junga ran down the stairs. Though wounded, he knocked as many people out the way as he could. He tossed bags of cocaine out of his pockets. He realized the police would soon arrive, but little did he know as soon as he landed on the last stairs that he would be hit by another bullet from an officer's gun.

Before being shot, he was able to fire off a round of shots. One hit Officer Newman in the heart. Newman was dressed in plain clothes. He lay mortally wounded at the entrance of the building. Joey fell to the ground next to Newman. Their blood entwined into one big puddle. Paramedics rushed toward Joey once the crowd of clients emptied the building.

Halt! An officer dressed in plain clothes shouted. He quickly removed his shield and flashed it in full view to the frightened patrons of the drug den. Within minute's hordes of reporters gathered at the scene. The five o'clock news anchor for a major television station seemed to command attention. "This is Katy Sponal of Channel Five News Team–The smoke from the blazing guns has not yet cleared the air. Stay tuned for this fast breaking story."

Blue uniformed officers met them at the exit with guns drawn. People nearly tripped over Officer Newman and Joey. Newman had no pulse and Joey was seriously injured.

Pandemonium broke out across the police station as news of Newman's death spread. Chief Summerlyn slammed the door and shouted, "I'm not giving that thug a hero's funeral. Newman wasn't assigned to that case—he was a rogue cop. Newman sold drugs to purchase expensive art. He was directly involved in the sale of pirated art."

A faint pulse was found on Joey Junga. Emergency measures were taken to save Junga's life. Junga was rushed into the ambulance and transported to the nearest hospital. Emergency surgery was ordered. After five hours of surgery, the bullets that lodged in his spine and lower leg were removed.

Twenty-four hours after the sedative wore off, the police proceeded to the hospital to question him. Joey was stubborn. He refused to answer any questions.

"Junga, how were you involved in the Pention murder?"

Junga refused to answer. "Where's my lawyer? I'm in pain."

The officers stopped the questioning until he was able to contact his lawyer. Joey responded in a hoarse voice, "Come back another day. We did not get our supply yet." He quickly fell back to sleep. It seemed as though he was not totally cognizant of his surroundings. Joey was a master of disguise and escape. Joey faked that response to throw everyone off.

He knew that he needed a lawyer. Even in excruciating pain, he was able to hold his own until he could contact his lawyer.

Upon awakening the next morning Joey realized he was paralyzed.

"Nurse, nurse" screamed Joey. He managed to buzz the bell to contact the nurse.

"Call the doctor. I can't move, and I need to call my lawyer."

Joey's lawyer, John Emory, was well-known in lawyer circles. He was a professional criminologist and criminal lawyer who represented many criminals. He worked in the police department for many years before changing careers. After three years of night school, Emory graduated with high honors from Fordham University Law School.

Emory's client list included high-profile criminals. Emory represented Pention on many occasions.

"I am Junga's attorney. Put Summerlyn on the phone." The dispatcher knew Emory's name and quickly transferred the call to Summerlyn. "Under no circumstances are you to question Junga until I am able to come to the hospital."

"Now that we have that straight, I will arrive at 1:00 p.m. today," said Emory. Emory did not take no mess. Mr. Emory questioned Junga briefly.

When the police arrived, Emory advised them that his client was not in any condition to respond to questions at this time. The police advised Emory that he was being charged with the murder of Pention, the murder of Officer Manley, and the attempted murder of an unidentified man. Police retrieved the gun at the scene of the crime and tested it for a match. The bullets matched the bullets that were removed from the body of Pention.

"I need your client to answer one question." He turned to Junga. "How do you plead?"

"I plead not guilty. I'm not going down without a fight. Only a fool would admit guilt." Joey moaned in pain. Emory noticed that Joey's physician entered the room. "I'm sorry, Officer, we will have to hold off on that for the moment." Joey had not been advised of his medical condition.

"Joey, I'm sorry we tried, but—we were unable to repair the damage to your spine. You will be paralyzed from the waist down."

Joey hollered, "Nooo—!" His clangorous cry was heard in the hospital corridor.

Judgment Day

DURING THE PRELIMINARY HEARING, THE Judge set the bail at one million dollars. Joey was shocked. "What, are you kidding? I can't even walk anymore."

"That's right, most members of drug cartels have bail set at five million dollars. Because you are in a wheel chair, I reduced the bail amount."

Junga's lawyer advised him that this case was damn near impossible to defend.

Emory said, "You killed a cop. Based on this latest crime, you could easily face life in prison. It would be in your best interest to cooperate."

Junga admitted to his involvement in the crime and indicated that he knew the whereabouts of the third person. Emory advised Junga that the judge might consider a lesser sentence if he disclosed the name of the person or persons involved in this crime. "You should disclose any details that you know about the crime."

Junga was not at all happy with his lawyer's suggestion. He was livid. He demanded that his lawyer leave the room immediately. "Get out—!"

Emory turned around and walked quickly toward the door. His heels rang loudly on the freshly polished floor. "Come back Emory, you are right. There's no way out this time."

Emory said, "The Feds might grant you lenience if you provide them with information that leads to the apprehension of assailants."

"I was on my way up. Soon I would be recognized as a captain in the Mexican Pacifico Sur cartel. When I was a teenager, I was recruited into the cartel as a petty hustler of drugs. I stood on corners and sold drugs in the community. Most of my sales involved the sale of marijuana. We were in the midst of a tremendous turf war. We are the second biggest drug cartel in Mexico.

In order to advance, we had to bump off Pention. To put it in simple terms, Pention was like the general in the Zeta cartel. That's a major hit. You got to earn your way up the scale. "Pention was my idol. I studied his climb up the ladder. He earned his way up by making hits on a number of high ranking officers in other cartels. The unnamed man in the museum was part of our cartel. His name is Ian Jackson. He had knowledge of Jill's employment at

Omari Boutique. While enjoying the food at the café at Omari Boutique, he noticed Jill's ability to mingle with the patrons with ease. Once Jackson observed the collection at Omari, he contacted the cartel and suggested that they expand their operation to include art theft. Almar was a member of our cartel. Jackson was involved in the elaborate scheme to kidnap the owners."

Ian was assigned to the recruitment team. Junga informed the police that Ian tried to recruit Jill for the cartel. Jackson noticed her a few times when he visited the boutique. He figured she was a single mother with two small children who might need a better paying job. She was sexy and intelligent. Jackson decided he would recruit her for a highly lucrative position in the organization. Jackson planned to pay her a six-figure salary. They grossed over a billion dollars a year.

"They planned to ask Jill to redirect shipments to their warehouse. The organization needed to infiltrate Omari Boutique so that they could develop a highly skilled art napping team."

Jill sat in the perfect position to assist in their operation. She just had to withhold some of the client's information from Omari and funnel a list of potential clients to the organization. She was not going to have to get her hands dirty. Nor would she be directly tied to the drug activities. They use all types of tactics to recruit personnel.

"Sometimes individuals who fail to yield the call, well let's just say it can be dangerous. Jill was lucky. The cartel stopped pursuing Jill once they realized that she was married to a high profile lawyer."

Junga went on to say that Pention, a high-level drug dealer, was in their way. They wanted to take over his operation. In doing so, they would also assume his territory—a territory currently occupied by the Zeta cartel.

"We tracked him to the address and ambushed him. He was going to pick up a large supply of drugs there. He distributed the drugs to the various drug dealers in the country and to their international distribution centers. Our intentions were clear. We were there to rip him off. That's how we earn our stripes. I told you, killing was a guaranteed promotion in the cartel. Ian Jackson stabbed him. Gonzalez, a well-known drug dealer for our cartel, was there. He was the driver and acted as a lookout. After Jackson stabbed him, I shot him. It appeared as though Pention was already dead. I just put the icing on the cake. I shot him in the head.

"Ian noticed a lady looking at him from across the street. She seemed to realize that something was going on. I flung the gun out of my hand, ditching it in some nearby bushes. We escaped into the waiting car. During the struggle, Pention tried to escape from the car, tripped, and broke his leg. Jackson stabbed him in the groin while he was in the car. He severed a main artery.

Ian was a member of the Fuerzas Armadas de Mexico. "The Mexican Army's thirst for blood led to the development of an army of men trained to kill at whim. Ian was trained by them. He was a member of an elite covert operations unit of the Mexican Army. Ian was highly intelligent. Ian's father was a former member of the cartel. He followed in his father's footsteps.

"Jackson was assigned to a special mission in Florida because he was their soldier. If anyone could ensure that the drug shipment arrived and was delivered without intervention by the government, it was Jackson. Jackson's travel arrangements were set. He is scheduled to arrive at JFK airport at 5:00 p.m. He was given specific details and instructions."

Because of Junga's tip, the police intercepted the cartel's plan. Officers assigned to the case were advised that Ian Jackson was enroute to JFK airport, and he was carrying a large shipment of drugs on the plane.

Junga's lawyer recorded the conversation. He phoned the police immediately and advised them that his client was willing to share important information that would lead to a major break in the case of Pention. Junga divulged that, in addition to receiving a high rank in the cartel, he was awarded 2.4 million dollars to kill Pention and retrieve the stolen art from Omari Boutique and a well-known art gallery in Italy. Pention was guaranteed an additional $500,000 if succeeded. Pention dropped the ball. You can see, Pention did not complete the second part of the job. His accomplices also received a nice payday.

"Emory phoned Summerlyn to advise the department that Junga has decided to cooperate in the Pention investigation. Of course, we expect the Judge to consider a bargain on this matter. I have a signed confession from Junga and will provide the department with information that pertains to the murder." Summerlyn was in shock. Summerlyn yelled into his cell phone, "Det. Swoop, I need you now. This case is much bigger than we anticipated. Almar is also attached to this case. We have already notified the FBI."

The unit immediately met with Junga's lawyer. Assignments were given to various personnel in the department. A team was quickly put together to seize the drug shipment. Summerlyn thanked Det. Swoop for assisting in the resolution of the case. "As promised, here is the $20,000 check plus your hourly rate."

Summerlyn ran out the door. Squad cars were dispatched to the airport. A Port Authority police team was on the move. Marine helicopters were ordered. Officers were advised to observe Jackson's actions before moving in on him. They hoped to observe his pick-up points and then follow him to a possible drug factory. Agents in California advised local personnel that Jackson had boarded the plane as planned. The captain announced over the loud speaker that flight number 562 was expected to arrive on time. The current temperature in New York City was seventy degrees.

"Our suspect is wearing a Hawaiian shirt, jeans, and sneakers. He looks like a tourist."

The police spotted Jackson as he departed from the plane. They were advised to tail him. They sent a number of unmarked cars to follow his trail. Unbeknown to Jackson, the unmarked cars included a number of SUVs that carried an arsenal of surveillance equipment.

Upon arrival at JFK, Jackson went to the baggage claim. He then ordered a rental car. The FBI remained unnoticed by Jackson. He made a quick stop in Bridgeport and then he drove to Massachusetts. He had no clue that a number of tails were on top of him. His final stop was on the waterfront in Boston, near Faneuil Hall. A man in a pinstriped suit awaited his arrival. Jackson walked toward him with a small paper bag in his hand. A quick exchange occurred between Jackson and the man. Unknown to the undercover team, the guy he met was Gonzalez. Gonzalez wore a finely tailored gray pinstriped suit with a tailored white shirt and a paisley tie. When Jackson left, he did not have the brown bag in hand. Jackson placed a note inside with instructions regarding the pick-up spot for the large drug delivery. A couple of bags of cocaine were placed inside the bag. Gonzalez had a large appetite for coke.

Undercover men caught the transaction on their camera. Jackson and the suited man sat outdoors in a secluded area of the riverfront outdoor cafe. After a brief bite of food and around of cocktails, Jackson placed the paper bag on the table.

"After you complete the job, Jackson, you'll receive that bulk payment we promised you—five hundred thousand dollars. Your next delivery spot is in Hartford. I'm leaving your payment in the tip and payment book; just leave a tip for the waiter. The rest is yours."

The suited man left with the bag. Jackson left a rather large tip in the leather money holder. He charged the restaurant bill to a bogus credit card so that his trail could not be traced. Not a bad payday, for the waiter who knew Jackson for many years.

Before he departed from the parking lot, Jackson quickly thumbed through the money. Gonzalez paid Jackson a thousand dollars in cash and included a cashier's check made out to him in the amount of five thousand dollars.

The police and the FBI immediately surrounded the area. The sound of NYC Harbor police helicopters could be heard overhead. The crowd was somewhat thin. The FBI busily searched their database in an attempt to identify him. The suited man was on the FBI's most wanted list. His name, according to their database, was Juan Gonzalez.

A small circle of shields, held in the hands of the officers, extended toward the suited man who walked away from the bistro table. All that was left on the plates was the crumbs from the food they had eaten.

Gonzalez remained oblivious until a number of plainclothes officers ordered him to halt, with their guns drawn. He was cornered like a wild animal in a zoo cage, waiting for his zookeeper to free him.

Jackson noticed the developing scene and tried to flee. He ran north but was immediately met by three undercover officers and the FBI.

"FBI— Freeze! You are under arrest for the sale of illegal drugs," echoed through the air.

Jackson and Gonzalez surrendered. They were handcuffed and placed in protective custody.

The drug supply, as well as Jackson's and Gonzalez's cars were confiscated and immediately impounded. A note inside the bag indicated that the rest of the supply will arrive the next day at Logan International Airport at 7:00 a.m.

"These men are connected to the Pacifico Sur cartel," said the captain. Ian Jackson had a number of outposts in different states. His primary post was located in Atlanta. Atlanta's prime location and extensive transportation system included one of the largest airport hubs, therefore shipment to other areas was easy.

Summerlyn praised Det. Swoop. "It is highly unusual to crack a case like this in record time, as you did. Our department wants to recognize you in a public ceremony. Sometimes they say that timing is everything, but I believe skill is also a contributing factor. Obviously, your skills are superior. We thank you."

Det. Swoop phoned Omari Boutique to advise Susan and Omari that he had information on the case that he would like to share with them. Omari held the phone close to his ear as he listened to Det. Swoop's raspy voice on the phone.

"That is fabulous, Det. Swoop. I just hope it is good news."

"Can you come into the office tomorrow, Omari, with Jill, Leon, and Susan?"

"Not a problem," said Omari. "Three o'clock works for us. I'll close the boutique early."

When they arrived at the station, Det. Swoop informed them that they could finally rest their minds. He turned to Jill. "Ian Jackson, a high ranking member of the Pacifico Sur drug cartel followed you in the museum and was responsible for placing those unwanted calls to you."

"He noticed Jill at Omari Boutique. The cartel expanded their operations to include art theft. Omari Boutique was targeted. Ian Jackson was going to recruit you Jill. He thought you were single with two young children and might jump at the opportunity to receive a nice payday.

Jill was shocked. "That man was trying to recruit me? Me…me. I have never participated in criminal activity."

"They wanted you to be the inside gal in the boutique. They wanted you to withhold potential customers from Omari Boutique. These customers would be redirected to the cartel's art boutique. After a while, they intended to offer you a position as a receptionist in their office."

"What—?" said Jill, "You've got to be kidding!" "Why people would entertain the thought of involving themselves in a lifestyle that is crooked was beyond Jill's comprehension. "It's a hard walk, I would imagine— walking on the wrong side of life."

Det. Swoop concurred. "Yes, but perhaps the most difficult thing in today's world is to walk around the bad ones and remain unscathed. Once they realized you were married to a high-profile lawyer, they scrubbed that thought."

Leon said, "Thank God I returned home from the reserves when I did."

After they departed from his office, Det. Swoop looked out the window of his brownstone office and quietly thought, *it turned out to be a nice day. It seems the doves have a message. As I drove down the street today, I saw three brown doves walking on the street. Doves symbolize peace.*

BOOK TWO

Justice Is Blind

"SUSAN, I AM SO BLESSED to have found a woman like you. When I reflect upon my life, I reminisce about the happy times in my life—growing up in a suburb just outside of New York City, spending summers in Pennsylvania watching cows graze on the moss-green grass from the porch of my grandmother's house. Grandpa was the founder of Union Baptist Church in New Salem, Pennsylvania. How ironic. No one would have thought that my strong Baptist upbringing would ultimately lead to a career as a gospel singer. Sometimes I return to the house in Mount Hope. Occasionally, I stumble onto a pile of old newspapers tossed haphazardly on the neatly manicured lawn.

Memories of family gatherings remain in my mind. Cookouts on the flagstone patio brought our friends and relatives home to laugh about the good old days. Yes, life was grand. Security did not knock on the door to tell you to turn your music down. When you come from a musical family, music is your life. The volume control was always on full blast when Dad was home. Music seeps into your bones and fills your soul. Mom and I laughed like there was no tomorrow. Mom told me that she used to act like a minister when she was a child. Who knows? Perhaps it was a prophetic vision of my destiny. Mom was funny. Mom never missed a day of Sunday school. She was steadfast in her belief in God. Dad, on the other hand, well I do remember him repeating one Bible verse: 'Jesus wept.' "Weeping is what I do. You see, Susan, when I am moved by the Holy Spirit I cry."

"My brother and I were born on the same day. Harry is thirteen years older than me. They call that scotch twins. He used to tickle me to death. I remember screaming at the top of my lungs, 'Harry, stop.' He refused to listen. Than one day, he tickled me so hard that I fell down to the floor. I thrashed around on the floor and ended up breaking the living room floor lamp. Of course, Mom had a bout with angry when she arrived home to see the lamp was shattered. My grandmother told me that she went to the store one day, and when she returned home to the semi-attached coal miner's house, I was soaking wet. My brother squirted me with water from the hose that was used to water the lawn."

"All I can say is, some things never change. We were total opposites. I came to realize that my brother did not know my mom. He was shocked to find out that Mommy loved to dance. He discovered that when she was in the nursing home. He was so removed from the family. I tell you, wonders never cease to amaze me. My brother incorrectly reported my grandmother's maiden name on my mother's death certificate." Omari shook his head and laughed.

"My brother was very rarely home. Family was secondary. The streets and the girls grabbed a hold of him. The highest grade he ever got was an A in sex education, and he majored in sex education for the rest of his life. He was the peep show movie projectionist on Forty-Second Street.

The one thing he instilled in me that saved me from a life of drug and alcohol abuse occurred in my teens. As usual, I was entertaining myself in my bedroom. He came to my bedroom with a paper bag, opened it, and said, 'You see this? This is weed. Don't ever touch it.' Can't say I never touched it, but I thank God that I never became a prisoner to weed, alcohol, or other drugs.

Perhaps the wildest escapade I experienced with Harry occurred when I in my twenties. Harry asked me to ride with him to the Bronx in his fully loaded, mint green Buick Electra. That car was bad. Till this day, I still swear by the smooth ride of an American built car. One could hit a major pothole and hardly feel the impact.

He drove somewhere in the South Bronx and ordered me to stay in the car while he went to some unknown location. I was just happy to be out with my big brother. He parked the car about a half-block away from the store and told me to remain in the car. I wasn't sure where he went, but knew he would return. I later learned that his friend's liquor store was located there. I sat in the car and listened to music. Then I suddenly heard a loud pop and screaming. Two black men in the not-too-far-distance stood on the sidewalk. I noticed a man hopping on one foot on the sidewalk. I jumped into the driver seat and flew out of there. As I drove by, I saw the guy hopping on the sidewalk and noticed a guy running away from the scene of the crime.

"I flew past him in the car while looking at him from a distance in the rear-view mirror. I was not exactly sure where Harry went. Then I saw the liquor store and thank God my brother was standing outside. I opened the car door. First thing he said when he got in the car was, 'Did you see that? That guy shot a guy in the foot.' I quickly responded, "Yes." 'That guy just walked up to him and shot him in his foot.'"

Harry got in the car, I drove like a bat out of hell. Once we escaped, I forced Harry to drive the car. Harry knew all the ins and outs of all the streets in Queens, the Bronx, and Manhattan. He got behind the driver's wheel and wheeled us back home. I was young and none—the-wiser until one day I woke up.

"Yesterday was cool. Peace signs filled the air, and people were united. Hippies and flower children ruled—not gangster rap. There were no gunshots. A child shot dead from a stranger's bullet was unheard of. School massacres and the glorification of violence are totally out of control. AIDS and homeless shelters were nonexistent. Rents were affordable and career growth was a given. We were not locked in a box spinning around in circles. When does the senseless killing of innocence stop? How do we save the children? How do we change a system that is engulfed in injustice?

"The system has been abused, misused and turned into a mangled statue with a never ending chain of madness. Seems like the criminals are now the victors, Susan." Omari shook his head in disbelief.

I became a victim of the very system I worked for. When I became, homeless it was surreal. Felt like I had infiltrated the homeless system. I envisioned the newspaper headlines: *Former Caseworker Becomes Resident at a Homeless Center, Investigates the System.* Ironically, I became homeless when I was forced out of my rightful inheritance because of an illegal deed change. I got a first-hand glance of poverty, welfare, and pride in work, and I witnessed the failure of our system to recognize the voice of a well-seasoned pro.

"Justice is blind. That scale is standing straight up in the air. The coins have fallen to the ground. Even a child can see. An incompetent person is not of sound mind and cannot be deemed competent when diagnosed with dementia. They cannot be held accountable for their actions. There was no way in hell my mother would have signed the title of the house. My mom had dementia when the deed to the house was changed. But the twist is this story is that my mother and I had the same exact name until her death. In fact, she was in the nursing home's dementia and Alzheimer's care unit."

A two-dollar piece of paper can sure create havoc in one's life and force the innocent victim to spend thousands of dollars to force the sale of the property."

"You see, Susan, I took a walk with Jesus, and the devil came a running with his team of professional players."

"You know I know, Susan, the rain will come as we walk on life's undefined journey."

"The sun will not always shine," Susan responded. "Be grateful."

"Trust me, I am grateful. They say there is no peace when there is no justice, said Omari."

Susan responded, "No truer words have been spoken."

Susan was never content with accepting the leftovers and crumbs from the table. That just was not written in her dictionary, nor instilled in her by her parents. "I have rights, and there are legal eagles out here. Their job is to defend our rights when laws and constitutional rights are denied."

Omari nodded. People like Martin Luther King Jr. stood up for our rights, and I am in tune with his message. Doors were opened because some refused to be complacent. Only the strong survive. This world is so full of darkness that when the light shines, the clouds cover the sunlight. I have always been a freedom fighter. As a child, I refused to sign the petition to stop school busing. I think I was in the third grade when that occurred. I attended a classmate's party. During the festivities, the president of the PTA wanted me to sign the petition.

"Thank God I refused to sign the petition." A child's name does not belong on a petition without parental knowledge and permission. Oddly enough, that was my first taste of corruption.

There are blocks, bricks, stones, and barricades to dreams. In my opinion, everyone should be able to achieve their dreams without interruption. I am so happy I met you, Susan. Civil rights gains made have been eroded. Didn't they know their history?"

We have become a society that allows criminals to walk. That is why crime statistics are so high. The officials do not heed the cries of the victims. Grace, they say, just will not let you do wrong. Well, I am full of grace, and the lesson that is crammed down my throat is there is no justice for those of us who stand on principle.

"They come like thieves in the night, scavengers jumping on an opportunity to reap financial gain, lacking compassion or moral conviction."

Susan interjected, "Omari, the bible says 'The Lord shall send the rod of thy strength out of Zion: rule thou in the midst of thine enemies.'"

"Susan, can you see? Life is twisted in the wrong direction. If each of us took the time to try to pull someone up, what a beautiful society we would live in. Perhaps I am lost in my own reality, for today's story has a different tune. I hear a sour note ringing in my ear. I see the hands of time being turned backward, rotating counter-clockwise."

"In the old days, your word was your bond. Today we are like papers blowing in the wind. Living in a robotic state, lacking feelings— and that is not what we are here for. We are human beings who bleed hurt and cry. Can't you see, Susan, I endured a rape—a rape of my fortunate, passions, family, and dreams—until I found you. Perhaps the worst crime is relative against relative. The powers that be don't want to venture into that arena. But the law does not read 'excluding blood.' Sibling and family abuse are real. I was born to dream, and those dreams are my reality. I didn't reach for crumbs. I aimed for the galaxy where stars are born and cultivated.

"Finding a woman who realized the power of dreams has made my life complete. Where would I be if it weren't for you, Susan? I love you with all my heart."

"I have a master's degree, and now they say I am over-qualified. 'Lord Jesus, please caste this boulder to the side,' is what I prayed for."

"Some of these companies have failed. It's no wonder that many of the young college students are moving to the Orient to pursue their dreams. A happy employee is more likely to excel and go above the call of duty and produce positive results that will lead to increased revenue and productivity."

"I think I'll start the stop-the-backward-rotation movement. As they say in the movement, "Never backwards always forward." Used to be a time when you went to college, you graduated, climbed, and gradually advanced. Stepping stones can turn into a nightmare. Watch out for the stepping-stone jobs. But when forced onto welfare and you know you were not supposed to be there, you take whatever comes your way to get off. Get off is what I did. They coded me as a high school graduate while I was on welfare.

"I had years of experience as a senior caseworker, but the employment counselor said, 'Do not expect to make what you once made.' If they pulled the files, they would see that many senior caseworkers were hired provisionally, while I was forced to eat at soup kitchens and learn how to adapt to $16.75 every two weeks. Food stamps went a mighty long way. I swear Susan that is the truth. Pride in work— I did not need pride in work. I was the king of two jobs. I became a prisoner of a system that just could not see or should I say they chose not to see?

"It became a system built on greed. New parties sprung up and the new rule was lacking in emotion, social concern and failed to implement rules. When they forced me out my rightful inheritance, I nearly became the victim of police brutality. I was lucky. I did not know there were two officers in the house, Susan. One officer said I could get some items out of the house, so I went upstairs. Of course, I was upset but I was not aggressive. I admit I yelled, 'I can't believe this is going down like this.'" The officer took out his handcuffs, and I, who never backed down from a challenge, said, 'You threatening me? You better put down those handcuffs.' Thank god the officer complied. I was lucky."

It's had been fifteen years since Omari began his faith walk. He had stood up for his rights but he had to fight an unjust battle without weapons. They say that is the mark of a true warrior.

"Lord Jesus, please wake me up—this is not real. My mother and grandmother believed in civil rights. The NAACP was a common household name. They went to the March on Washington. I remember being mad when I was told that I could not go. My grandmother said, 'We don't know if we will return.' I was too young to comprehend those simple words. I was only five years old. They made me stay with an old lady who lived in the patch in Buffington, Pennsylvania, while my mother rode on a bus to Washington DC from New York, and my grandmother rode on a bus from Pennsylvania. That's where my grandma lived. "Justice, does it take on a different meaning in the twentieth century? Artists have a vision that escapes some. Some think light-years ahead of time."

Susan nodded her head yes and continued to snap fresh green beans in the kitchen.

"Marvin Gaye was way ahead of his time, Susan. 'What's going on?'—those words hold true today. How can we close our eyes to a system that is broken? Justice unattained can turn into a scratched record, burnt and warped in the sun. I tell you, Susan. See this photo here on the cover of this book. Well you can color it me—Upside down in America."

Susan, "I have experienced modern-day slavery and backward rotation that threatens to destroy the likes of many. There's no order in today's society. Justice is not reserved to a set few. I refuse to go to my grave without tasting the fruits of my labor. Justice will prevail. I never wanted for anything. Pinch me because this just is not real. Baked chicken served with macaroni and cheese, collard greens and sweet potatoes sure has a mighty fine taste. When I was a kid, my father purchased the whole side of the cow. The refrigerator was never void of food. But not too long ago, I experienced hunger pains. That's not the life I knew. Food was plentiful, and life was grand when I was a child. "

Omari shouted out, "They are stealing everything. Next they will steal my hair—and I don't have any hair." Omari bent down and pointed to his shiny bald head.

Susan laughed. "Please stop, Omari. My stomach is hurting from all of this laughter. I think you have missed your calling. You should enroll in acting classes. I can easily see you starring in a one man show."

Today, Susan and Omari are known throughout the world. Their art jazz boutique gallery has expanded. They now offer franchise opportunities and changed the name to the Omari Boutique for Arts and Jazz Café. Omari Boutique in now located in New York and New Jersey. Yesterday, a gentleman applied for an Omari Boutique for Arts and Jazz Café franchise. He wants to open a franchise in Atlanta, Georgia. Omari convinced the young entrepreneur to develop a franchise in Richmond, Virginia. He informed the applicant that Omari Boutique for Arts and Jazz Cafe will pay the re-location costs. It was an offer that the applicant could not refuse.

"Susan, my love," said Omari, "Success did not come easy, but look where we are now. We are the king and queen of Omari Boutique. Soon our star will shine. Our hands have been unshackled. The locks have finally opened. The chains have fallen off. Now we can prance lively on the golden sands of Maui."

So many people could see that Susan and Omari were madly in love.

Susan listened intently. Slowly her anger grew. She grabbed Omari's hand as she made a mad dash out the door.

"Where are we going, Susan?"

"Don't ask questions just get in the car, Omari."

Omari obeyed her orders. Susan drove haphazardly up the Major Deegan, forcing cars out her way that impeded her path.

"Where are we going?"

Susan eventually responded, "To your mother's house."

"What for?" asked Omari. Susan did not respond.

Omari became scared of Susan's out of the ordinary behavior, so he decided to text Jill. The text read: "Where are you, Jill?"

Jill responded in text: "I'm in the Bronx. I am @ Karen's house, TTUL."

Omari quickly replied to Karen's text: "No TTUL. I need you to drop what you are doing."

We just passed the Fordham Road exit in the Bronx. Omari texted: "Please drive to house where my mother once lived immediately." Jill replied: "Okay, CYA!"

"Karen, I have an emergency. That was my boss. I have to leave."

Afrolena threw her black slip-on shoes on her feet and ran out the door to her car. She drove so fast that she eventually caught up to them.

Susan must have been driving eighty miles per hour. She arrived at the house in record time. The small three-bedroom house— a home that once housed Omari, his mother, and his father—was located on a quiet dead-end block. Susan immediately noticed that the house appeared to be vacant. A puzzled look of bewilderment and shock appeared on Omari's face. The Roman shades that once covered the wooden framed windows were no longer there.

Susan abruptly departed from the top-of-the-line black Mercedes Benz. She noticed a rock that was the size of a baseball lying by the curb.

Omari noticed Susan's attraction to the rock. "Susan, you know I don't condone violence." She did not care what Omari said.

"Susan, please don't."

"Today, Omari— I don't care what you have to say— today I am forcing the hand of justice." She quickly bent down to the ground and picked up the rock. Susan firmly planted her two fingers on the rock that was the size of a baseball. Before Omari could grab her arm to stop her, Susan threw the rock into the window with all her might.

The impact of the rock hitting the living room window led to an avalanche of clear glass, splattering on the neatly manicured lawn. The loud crash of glass resonated throughout the neighborhood. The sound of police sirens could be heard in the not-too-far distance.

"Come on, Susan. Let's get out of here before the police arrive."

Susan appeared to be in a trance.

"Susan, come on, let's get out of here."

"No, Omari, leaving is not an option."

Omari's painful look of shock was painted firmly on his face. The sounds of the police sirens drew closer to them. Omari noticed that an entourage of police cars quickly pulled into the normally quiet block. A crowd of people gathered. One person in the crowd pointed her finger at Susan and shouted, "She did it."

Omari stood quietly on the side of the curb with tears streaming down his cheeks. Jill appeared to be a part of the police entourage because she arrived at the house right behind the police, ran out the car slamming the door behind her. "Oh my god what happened?"

"You have the right to remain silent." One officer handcuffed Susan. "You are under arrest for criminal trespassing and vandalism." Susan remained quiet. She was escorted to the police car by two police officers. Susan defiantly sat in the back seat of the squad car with her hands cuffed behind her back. She twisted and turned, trying to find a comfortable position so that the cuffs would not squeeze her wrists.

She eventually blurted out, "The time is now. I demand that you take these shackles off me now. Yes, I threw a rock at the living room window with my nonviolent hands, but you see officers, I did it to make a statement and create a scene that would finally lead to a full investigation on a crime that was never recognized. Omari and I are one. When Omari hurts, I hurt. Seems like no matter how much he screamed, he received no justice on a case that could have been solved with a twenty-five cents phone call year ago."

"The only way we were going to gain the attention of the officials was to commit a petty crime. Now you can see," shouted Susan. "The petty crime of throwing a rock into that window takes precedence over falsifying a deed."

Omari stood on the sidewalk with cell phone in hand. His phone rang.

"Hello, this is Ted Manley of WCDX radio." Omari responded to the media inquiries with haste. "Yes, Susan decided that enough is enough. Yes, it was an extreme action. However, my peaceful cries for help fell upon deaf ears. She knew my pain. I don't condone violence." Tears continued to stream down his face as he watched his queen about to be arrested and driven down the street in the blue-and-white squad car. The sight of his queen shackled in chains of iron was too much for him to bear."

In a broken voice, Omari informed Ted Manley of WCDX radio, "Sometimes you have to break the rules to receive attention. This issue has been going on since 2001. Lord knows I'm weary. Even Pope Francis has instructed his flock to break the rules. Susan is the love of my life. She and I are one."

"Officer, I'm standing up for the love of my life. That was his inheritance and somebody stole my computer art. Why don't you look into that officer? The house was fully paid for. The house still has his name on it, but he does not condone that. All of Omari's cries for help met upon deaf ears." Susan's voice shook as she spoke.

As the police car pulled further away, Susan screamed out to Omari from the open window, "Justice lost in a sea of pain will finally beat its way into the hall of justice." She quickly blew a kiss to Omari before the officers rolled the automatic windows up.

Susan, was promptly placed to the police station. "Omari is entitled to half the proceeds of that house."

A number of people converged. The multi-racial crowd consisted of approximately thirty people. They built a strong wall of video cell phones to record the incident. Jill shouted, "Power to the people." The crowd walked down the street behind the police cruiser that carried Susan. They turned onto Sheridan and marched down Prospect Avenue to the police station.

A number of people joined in the march. Some chanted, "No justice, No peace!" while others pumped their fists. People of all colors, shapes, ages and sizes pumped their fist high in the air. The chant was so loud that people from other blocks in the area were drawn to the scene. As they walked up the block, they too felt the aura of this uprising. "Voters' rights are here to stay."

An elderly man shouted, "Stop the stealing! Stop the violence."

This quiet dead-end block suddenly turned into a public demonstration and protest march for justice.

Omari decided to park his car and join the march. He and Jill led the march to Mount Hope City Hall. Omari reached into his pocket and called his lawyer. "I'm in the midst of leading a protest march to Mount Hope City Hall. Susan is in trouble. Contact the best civil right rights lawyer too. I'll explain this in detail when you arrive."

"The lawyer responded, "No problem—I'll be there in twenty-minutes."

The crowd of thirty grew to a crowd of hundreds, as neighbors from the various apartment buildings and private houses joined in the march.

A woman shouted, "Women united will never be defeated." Sopranos, altos, and tenors joined together in an arousing majestic chant of protest. "Fight back get back." Members of other civil rights organizations joined in the protest. National Action Network, NAACP, December 12 Movement, the National Organization for Women, P.O.P., Women's Rights for Vocal Justice, Black Lives Matter, All Lives Matter, Artist United for Justice, Musicians Sing for Justice and a host of local grassroots organizations marched for justice.

A well-known community activist minister limped up the street to join the march. Years of walking on picket lines had taken its toll on his knees. He was no longer able to march long distances. But that did not stop him from engaging in peaceful rallies and marches. Sometimes he drove his car in marches. As he walked up the street he shouted, "power to the people, the people united will never be defeated, we won't go back—we will fight back." "If there ain't gonna be no justice, there ain't gonna be no peace."

News 12, CBS and a host of a popular radio show host and news reporters arrived. Bob Slade put on his news reporter hat. He broadcast the live protest march on the radio. Slade became overfilled with emotions. He dropped the mic on the ground so that he too could join in the march. Some news reporters interviewed the protesters as they walked the three miles to Mt. Hope City Hall. Some of the press members chanted, "First Amendment rights."

After leading the protesters to city hall, Omari arrived at the police station. His attorney greeted him at the front door of the police station with a well-known civil rights lawyer. Omari and the attorneys were led to the area where Susan was being held.

As they entered the room, they heard Susan say, "I admit I threw the rock into the window. That house was owned by his mother and father. While I realize that house is small compared to what we can afford, this is a violation of his civil rights. We are charging you with inciting to riot, penal code 240.08. It's a misdemeanor. There will be no jail time. The desk officer will give you a…

"What said Susan, I did not tell those people to develop a march. But it's about time. The citizens of Mount Hope need to rise up. According to the New York State

Constitution Article 1 Section 11, 'no person shall be denied the equal protection of the laws of this state or any subdivision thereof. No person shall, because of race, color, creed, or religion, be subjected to any discrimination in his or her civil rights by any other person or by any firm, corporation, or institution, or by the state or any agency or subdivision of the state.'" "Years ago it was reported that there were eighty illegal lockouts. We all need justice, not just words reported in a newspaper," said Susan.

"Furthermore," the civil rights lawyer interjected, "Susan is right. Don't you utter another word."

Susan refused to shut up. "Officer, I am not shutting up. This is a free country. Freedom of speech is in the constitution. We are here for justice. His parents purchased the small three-bedroom house with marble fireplace, wet bar and private backyard when Omari was in the twelfth grade. "Honey, I tried to stop you from throwing that rock. You know I am against any form of violent protest. I realize it was the ultimate act of unselfish love but please don't ever...'"

Susan slowly placed her hand on top of his lips. "Omari, I did it out of love."

They formed the largest impromptu march in the history of the Mount Hope. Susan's Out of Love march was a huge success. The police finally located her stolen art. Omari—well he finally won his multi-million-dollar lawsuit based on the grounds of an adverse possession and illegal lockout.

The crown of glory that Susan and Omari developed blossomed. Their vision was born from a "mustard seed of faith." Jill and Leon Sullivan partnered with Susan and Omari Thomas.

Omari's million-dollar bloody statue was finally returned to him. The investigation revealed that a new cook at Omari Boutique's Brooklyn cafe stole the million-dollar statue.

Omari informed the police that he suspected the cook was a thief.

"I fired him, he was always late and sometimes he appeared to be intoxicated. The statues disappeared shortly after he began working in the Brooklyn store."

Investigators interrogated the cook for hours. Finally, he admitted that he stole the statue. He sold the stolen statue to Pention for $200 so that he could support his drug habit. The cook is currently incarcerated in an upstate prison for selling drugs to an undercover police officer.

It took three days of training from the guest Musical Director Milton Davis to transform the *Change* choir. On September 7th the *Change* choir was aired on the *Triumph Awards Show* and on the Sept. 13th premiere episode of the *Next One Up*. Immediately following the live television broadcast, the switch-board lit up. Then the call that beat all calls came through.

"Hey, Rev, this is Pastor Donnie. I saw the *Change Choir* on the Triumph Awards, Rev. Al. That choir has a wonderful sound now. I want them to be at the television station on

Sept. 13th so that they can appear on the premiere of my new television show. I want to give them a contract with my record company." "Sharpton responded that sounds great!"

Sharpton and the choir were elated. None were aware that Pastor Donnie placed the call from a car that was parked outside of NAN's New York Headquarters. Donnie McClurkin slowly walked into the room. He surprised them. "Hello, I wanted to personally tell the choir that my producer and I have decided to feature the choir on my new television show, *Next One Up*. Ladies and gentlemen you are victorious."

Within two days they met privately with McClurkin. A few members of the choir sang a few bars of McClurkin's song "*We Are Victorious*" McClurkin praised them. "Get ready to put on your *Sunday Best* cause you are the first one up. "Who is the president of the choir?"

Jill responded, "We don't have a president."

"Your first assignment is to develop a board for the choir and you need a new name for the choir."

The group of seven renegades hurdled together. Within five minutes a representative from the choir emerged. "I am the president of the Victory choir; my name is Gwen. This is our destiny and nothing's going to stop us now."

The choir sang a loud harmonious verse of the song.

We are victorious, we are victorious

Nothing can conquer us, we are victorious

Somebody scream and say we are victorious!

"Stop," shouted Pastor Donnie. "Sing that verse again."

The choir sang the verse again.

"Bravo, I'm putting you on tour."

The entire choir cheered and shouted, We Are Victorious!"

Two months passed. No one knew what happened to the choir. Al Sharpton decided to call Pastor Donnie.

"Donnie where is the choir?" said Sharpton.

"I stole the choir from the Rx. That choir was too good. I'm putting them on tour. It was god Rev. Al I was at the drive thru pick-up window and suddenly Gwen from the Change choir was right behind me on the pick-up line at the Rx. I know she did not follow me because there is a blind spot. There's no way that she knew I was on line."

"Donnie, you stole my choir. How dare you steal my choir, Donnie."

"They're happy, Rev. Al. I swear it was God. The Victory choir is going on an all-expense paid trip to Africa next year. Their song is about to hit the air waves and I am putting the song into heavy rotation."

"Victory choir, Donnie?" I'm gonna show you a victory, Donnie. I'll see you in New York."

Donnie responded, "Oh yeah, we will see about that. Gwen is coming with me." Both of them slammed the phone down.

Within three weeks Donnie showed Sharpton who got the victory. The Victory children's choir and the Victory adult choir sang in a sold out concert at the Barclay's Center.

BOOK THREE

The Troubling of the Water

Jill's annual African fashion show fundraiser garnered the attention of well-known international models. Her daughter, Rose, became a featured model in the Omari Boutique fashion show and a star in a popular daytime television show for teenagers. Jill's son, Little Sean, excelled in school. He won a scholarship to NYU's undergraduate program for journalism.

Omari's sister, Renee, passed away suddenly. News of her violent death shocked all. She was at the height of her career. There was an endless horizon ahead of her. Just prior to her death she was chosen to play the part of Billie Holiday in a made for television movie. Who would have known that Renee's final chapter in life would resemble the final chapter of Billie Holiday's life?

"I am the legal next of kin, your Honor. My sister Renee died six months ago after a wild night of partying.

Unfortunately, Renee succumbed to the ills of the streets. She became a substance abuser, a well-kept secret. Her suspicious death made headlines on the major newspapers and television networks."

Renee was the most beautiful girl on earth. Her powerful voice and philanthropic endeavors would never be forgotten.

The people commemorated the life and times of Renee Thomas-Norman, world-known singer and violinist. Renee was gone but not forgotten. A crowd of people gathered in the private invite-only funeral service.

Renee's name was sprawled across the front pages of every well-known newspaper and television station. Reverend Norman summoned his minister of communications. "Reverend Norman I will handle it. I understand this is very difficult for you."

His famed minister of communications was once a well-known public relations representative in a prestigious firm. He immediately pressed forward with a press conference and formal statement regarding the death of Pastor Norman's wife.

"Pastor Norman is overwhelmed with sorrow. On behalf of Reverend Norman and the family, I present this statement to you— "I am saddened to hear that my wife's body was found stripped and beaten on the banks of the Hudson River. Unfortunately, my wife became entangled in a world that included alcohol abuse."

A voice in the background yelled drugs—they found cocaine in her blood stream. Reverend Norman stepped forward.

"The Lord has spoken to me today. Today, I speak to you out of love. I tried to hide the reason for her death from the public, but the Lord has spoken to me today. He has directed me to become an active crusader in the war against drug use. Despite numerous efforts to rehabilitate her, I eventually employed tough love. Tough love came in the form of a separation. I thank all for your support and congenial words of comfort during this trying time in my life. I hope that the person or persons who committed this heinous crime will voluntarily come forward. Details regarding her homecoming service will follow."

A strong fortress of uniformed police surrounded Reverend Norman. In the weeks to come, a few anonymous tips came into the police station. Renee attended a birthday party for one of her friends. The drinks flowed, and let's just say that the bathroom was constantly filled with party-goers. Renee staggered from the bathroom in her silver high-heeled stilettos onto the crowded dance floor.

Witnesses informed the police that Renee lit up the room when she entered the club. "She was dressed in a red mini dress with plunging V neck and low-cut back. The cowl neck back falls just above her buttocks. Renee's smooth brown skin and curvy hips seemed to rotate around the room. Her oversized hips and petite waist line could not be ignored. She was a human magnet that drew all men to her.

There's many meanings to the word swoop. In the *Urban Dictionary* a *swoop* is when a man moves in on a girl who has a man.

"That's what happened. Some smooth talking man stole my wife from me. I pulled my wife up. She was a recovered alcoholic."

"Renee always loved flowers, said Reverend Norman. Renee was never afraid to talk about dying. She always said, "honey please give me my flowers while I am alive."

A long pregnant pause of silence followed. Omari sung Renee's favorite funeral song, "I'll Fly Away." Renee's talented and now famous brother Omari lifted up the funeral with a solo that touched everyone's heart.

Little Flame aroused the mourners with her soulful rendition of "*Amazing Grace.*"

The minister began the eulogy. "It's always hard to watch a loved one die, but this particular death obviously affected me, but I know my wife wanted me to eulogize her. My wife of nearly ten years has been called home."

He could not contain his emotions. "I spoke to Renee that night. I told her 'don't go to the party.' Some of you devils need to be called out. I know who you are. Some of you sitting in this room today. Took my Christian wife down, the devil got a hold of her. Yes, some of you know that we have been separated for the past year, but she was the love of my life."

Reverend Norman was overcome with sorrow. Rev. Norman slowly handed the microphone to his Associate Pastor before he totally broke down in the pulpit. Prior to departing from the pulpit Pastor Norman proclaimed, "The Lord will prevail."

The final soloist Donnie McClurkin's melancholy voice emerged, "Soon and very soon we are going to see the King, hallelujah, hallelujah we're going to see the King." The Victory choir sung in the background. The funeral director slowly closed the casket—a sign that the service ended. The crowd of well-dressed dignitaries, relatives, friends and mourners slowly departed from the church.

Rev. Norman slowly walked to his black Mercedes Benz stretch limousine. He quietly informed a reporter who slipped through security, "Who would know that her life would end so tragically?" A stream of tears fell down upon Rev. Norman's cheeks. Rev. Norman's strong liberation voice suddenly disappeared. His quivering voice of sorrow slowly belted out, "soon we will see if justice prevails. No one is immune, no color, race, economic class and no religion is immune. I implore all of you to listen to the voice of the Lord. It seldom melts into a clear crystal river that rolls smoothly into a bountiful oasis of life. It drags others down and imprisons the very ones who love them. Stop the violence! Dare to say no to drug abuse!"

listen|imagine|view|experience

AUDIO BOOK DOWNLOAD INCLUDED WITH THIS BOOK!

In your hands you hold a complete digital entertainment package. In addition to the paper version, you receive a free download of the audio version of this book. Simply use the code listed below when visiting our website. Once downloaded to your computer, you can listen to the book through your computer's speakers, burn it to an audio CD or save the file to your portable music device (such as Apple's popular iPod) and listen on the go!

How to get your free audio book digital download:

1. Visit www.tatepublishing.com and click on the e|LIVE logo on the home page.
2. Enter the following coupon code:
   515d-8014-64ef-09ae-1242-5ce6-be85-447c
3. Download the audio book from your e|LIVE digital locker and begin enjoying your new digital entertainment package today!